BOOKS BY OLIVIA ASH

The Nighthelm Guardian Series

City of the Sleeping Gods

City of Fractured Souls

City of the Enchanted Queen

Demon Queen Saga

Princes of the Underworld

Wars of the Underworld

Mistress of the Underworld

Sentinel Saga

By Dahlia Leigh and Olivia Ash

The Shadow Shifter

The Demon Prince

The Rogue Alchemist

STAY CONNECTED

Olivia Ash occasionally takes over the Wispvine Publishing social media channels on Facebook, Instagram, and Twitter.

Olivia also likes to hang out with Lila Jean in their Facebook group specifically for readers like you to come together and share their lives and interests, especially regarding the hot guys from their reverse harem novels. Please check it out and join in whenever you get the chance! Everyone in there is amazing, and you'll fit right in.

https://www.facebook.com/groups/LilaJeanO-liviaAsh/

Sign up for email alerts of new releases AND exclusive access to bonus content, book recommendations, and more!

https://wispvine.com/newsletter/nighthelm-academy-email-signup/

Enjoying the series? Awesome! Help others discover The Nighthelm Guardian Series by leaving a review at Amazon.

http://mybook.to/Nighthelm1

CITY OF THE ENCHANTED QUEEN

BOOK THREE OF THE NIGHTHELM
GUARDIAN SERIES

OLIVIA ASH

BOOK DESCRIPTION

Once a guardian of the people, Sophia is now a wrongfully convicted fugitive of Nighthelm—and the hunt is on.

Deadly assassins stalk her every step, and the murderous creatures of the Witch Woods are hot on her heels. Nothing and nowhere is safe. Anyone brave enough to fight beside her risks a gruesome death.

Her only redemption is to restore the rightful heir to the throne—but the clock is ticking.

Though Sophia and her men barely escaped Ripthorn mountain with their lives, they must return. For deep in the mountain, the heir still lives... for now.

Enchantments, corruption, and assassins stand in Sophia's way.

As with so many things in this timeless city, not everything is as it seems. Old enemies resurface. Painful truths are unearthed. And the only way for Sophia to discover the truth behind her fractured magic is to end the Nameless Master's takeover… no matter the cost.

Edric is a master of war. Zeke, a master of magic. Andreas, a master of death. These men fear nothing but losing the woman they love—and though they would die for her, only Sophia can end the bloodshed.

For the truth is she's painfully familiar with the one responsible for the deep corruption in Nighthelm…

And she's closer to the lethal truth than even she realizes.

City of the Enchanted Queen is third reverse harem novel in the Nighthelm Guardian Series. Get ready for a breathtaking story, soulmate romance, lip-biting love scenes, mind-blowing magic, one kickass heroine, three gorgeous men, lots of toned muscles, fights to the death, and edge-of-your-seat action.

The Nighthelm Guardian series has now been extended! You now know what Sophia is, and why her soul was broken... but now you can discover who she really is, and the truth behind her mysterious blood-line. Stay tuned for books four through six, coming in Spring 2019!

CONTENTS

CHAPTER ONE

SOPHIA

*S*ophia peeled her eyes open. The blur of the morning was heavy in her eyes as she stretched. Andreas's arms wrapped tighter around her. She smiled, loving the way his arms felt around her body. Protective and warm. She inhaled his skin and caught the scent of a cooking fire nearby. Her stomach growled, demanding sizable portions of the fried meat and eggs. But she was so comfortable lying with Andreas. Part of her wanted to get more sleep, and part of her needed food.

"You appear to have a monster in your stomach," Andreas said, mumbling the words sleepily.

She looked up at him. His eyes were still closed, and his face was completely relaxed. She smiled. "Yeah. Seems so. But I'm too comfortable." She snuggled in closer.

Her stomach growled again. The thing seemed to have a mind of its own, demanding sustenance immediately.

Andreas chuckled and shifted. "Go eat. I'll be along in a moment."

She groaned as she forced herself to pull away from his warm embrace to ease the monstrous hunger in her belly. She stopped at the doorway and looked over her shoulder, finding Andreas had sat up and was tugging on a shirt, his tight muscles shifting with each movement. She bit her lip then peeked outside. The sun was bright and warm and danced along the canopy of the trees, turning the leaves a vibrant green.

As she stepped out of the hut she shared with her men, she found Ezekiel and Edric standing guard near the entrance of the village. She smiled at seeing them so serious and dutiful. Sophia grew even more appreciative of their presence. Having them around made her feel stronger and more in control. More complete. This life would be impossible to bear without them, and she didn't know what she would do if she was ever faced with that day. They had taken permanent residence in her life. They were the missing pieces of her soul.

Her heart swelled as she realized that she was in love with them more than ever. She would do anything for them.

Nearly losing them in Ripthorn Mountain was as

close to losing them she ever wanted to get. Apart from Andreas, who didn't seem as affected as the other two, she practically watched them wither away. Though the trip wasn't all bad. Despite being betrayed by one of the creatures of the mountain, she managed to not only kill Lady Naomi and free the people the woman had enslaved, but her and her men defeated the vexsnare. The same creature that nearly killed her over a decade ago and was after Andreas, thanks to a curse from Tryce Klatrix. She also killed Winston for torturing her men and trying to enslave her. She could still feel his clammy hands on her skin from the number of times he touched her.

Good riddance.

A shiver trickled along her spine as she recalled his advances. Bile rose in the back of her throat. She washed it down with a long pull of water from the ladle.

Another thing that came from the mountain was her reliving the day she was broken and discovering that not only was the Nameless Master responsible for her becoming an *anima contritum*, but he was also after the Duchess of Westray, Steward of Nighthelm. Though she still really couldn't explain how she knew those things, she just *knew*. Information had flooded her mind as soon as she had relived the moment her soul was broken. She wasn't sure what the Nameless Master wanted with the duchess. Only that he was after her. Sophia wondered if the Nameless Master was also somehow responsible for the girl in the crystal coffin. It wasn't much of a connection, but everything else seemed to lead toward him.

Sophia needed to warn the duchess about the Nameless Master's plan to harm her, but how? The castle wouldn't let her in, and the Nighthelm army was still after them.

They needed a plan. But first, breakfast and checking in with Ezekiel and Edric. She decided to do the last part first. As she opened her mouth to say, "good morning," an arrow whizzed toward her. She twisted in the nick of time, narrowly missing the razor-sharp blade that was aimed at her heart. Jumping into action, she rushed forward and caught the one that would've landed in Ezekiel.

She quickly glanced at him. His eyes widened, and he nodded in thanks. She nodded as well and released Haris. "*Vocavi.*"

Green mist lifted from her arm and hovered just a few feet in front of her. As Haris solidified, Sophia dodged another arrow aimed at her head. The shot was close. She felt the fletching brush the top of her hair as it zipped over her. Haris instantly rushed into the fight.

A horn blasted through the camp, alerting the rest of the wraiths to the attack. Dozens of the shifters rushed forward, joining Sophia and her men in the battle. Even more attackers charged forward, outnumbering the wraiths, Sophia, and her men four to one. They were covered from head to toe, with no distinguishable features. Hoods covered their heads and they wore masks over their mouths.

Andreas shouted, "Assassins!"

She quickly charged toward an attacker and blasted it with fire. Pulling on her sword, she held it toward another assassin who crouched low and held two short swords aimed directly at her.

The sound of battle filled her ears behind her, and she wanted to quickly take this bastard out.

The dual-wielding assassin charged her, swinging his swords in rapid succession. Sophia kept up with the attacks, parrying and making an effort to disarm him or her, but she was forced backward with each of her opponent's advances. She pulled out her dagger and stepped up her game. Her magic seeped to the surface, coating her body in bright purple and blue sparks.

Before, this would've been cause for concern—but she was in control now, and she didn't have to worry about the possibility of losing hold of herself anymore. She smiled, calling upon the power within her, and she felt renewed strength. Her hits were harder, and her assassin was pushed back this time. She bent low and swung her leg out, intending to swipe the legs of her opponent from underneath him, but the assassin saw it coming and jumped into the air.

His movements mimicked that of the lynx creatures within the mountain. But having them on the surface didn't make much sense. Unless, they sought revenge against Sophia for killing their kind, like the grimms.

Regardless, she fought. And when the opponent showed zero signs of giving up, she held her hand out toward her assailant and released her magic in a beam of light that nearly blinded her. The person growled, all cat-like, and lashed out haphazardly. Sophia kicked the creature in its stomach and sent it flying back into a tree, impaled by a branch.

Turning, Sophia watched as another assassin sneaked up behind Edric while he faced off with two others.

Damn.

She ran, and the magic coursing through her started to burn. As the assailant lifted a dagger to plunge into Edric's back, she released a ball of fire, setting him ablaze. He dashed about, wailing, trying to douse the fire. She quickly ended his suffering by throwing her sword into his back.

Once she turned to take out yet another assassin, she found them escaping into the woods. Haris went to run after them.

"Haris, no!" Sophia called out. He stopped and gave

her a questioning look. She shook her head and he returned to her. She whispered, *"Reverte."*

His physical form dissolved into bright green mist and floated toward her and into her forearm. He was safe and with her.

Andreas said, "Come look at this."

Edric, Ezekiel, and Sophia joined him at one of the bodies of the assassins. He had pulled off the hood to reveal that they were, indeed, the lynx from the mountain.

"What do you make of this?" Andreas asked.

"That we pissed some people off in the mountain," Edric said and crossed his arms over his chest. "I don't think we will see much of them anymore."

Mica and Ozul joined the group. They stared down at the creature, scrutinizing every detail. Sophia almost shuddered.

"The bastards killed two of our own," Mica said. Ozul nodded.

Sophia said, "I agree that we pissed off someone, but this seemed more than just a revenge killing. I believe there is more behind it."

Ezekiel said, "If creatures have followed us from the mountain and found us here, there is no telling how long it will be before Nighthelm's guards locate us, or the grimms." He nodded at Sophia. "We need to consider if it is safe to continue staying here and jeopardizing more of the wraiths' lives."

Ozul snorted. "We are capable of handling ourselves. It takes a lot to kill us. Those two deaths were likely very lucky happenstance. Nothing more."

Andreas nodded. "I agree. And we have nowhere else to go. None of us can return to Nighthelm."

"Not to mention," Sophia added, "traversing Witch Woods has its own fair share of dangers. However, that won't stop me from finding the heirs."

Edric stood taller. "Then we should set up watch. Ezekiel, do you think you could line the village with some traps? Set a perimeter so that we are warned before another attack?"

Ezekiel nodded.

"I'll tend to the wounded," Sophia said.

Andreas said, "And I'll work with Edric to set up watches."

Sophia left to offer help to whoever needed it. Meanwhile, she thought about the chance that someone from the mountain had followed them out. She knew there was more to the attack. Someone was trying to stop them. But she wouldn't stop. She had a job to do, and she refused to even rest before that job was done.

CHAPTER TWO

SOPHIA

Once all the wounded were tended to, the watches set up, and Ezekiel had finished the wards, she and her men sat together enjoying a hot meal. She couldn't finish eating. Her mind was too occupied.

"We should make sure we capture one next time," Edric said. "For questioning."

"I agree," Sophia said. "This way we'll at least know who sent them and why."

The men nodded.

"Perhaps there are some additional supplies lying about that could be used to fortify the perimeter?" Ezekiel asked.

Andreas shrugged. "I don't see why not. There are a few huts that are vacant. You could always check them out."

Sophia stood. "I'll look in the huts. Anything I find I will bring to Mica or Ozul first."

"Good idea," Andreas said.

Sophia excused herself and went on her little hunt. At first, a lot of the huts didn't contain much of anything beyond a few weapons and armor. But in the last hut, she found a strange, enchanted chest. It appeared old, like it had sat there for a number of years just waiting to be found. Kneeling closer, she discovered there was a number of locks on it. Whoever this chest belonged to, he or she definitely didn't want anyone opening it. It probably had traps too. On the lid, just above a lock, was a familiar phoenix symbol. She couldn't begin to piece together where she knew it from. It was just there, tugging at the oldest of memories, calling to her.

Sucking in a breath, she brushed a finger over the symbol. Flashes of images rushed through her mind.

A woman held her... though she couldn't quite make out the woman completely, she hummed a soft lullaby as a tiny hand wrapped around her entire finger. She was safe. Things made sense.

It was such a sudden and powerful image that she jerked her hand back and stared at the chest for several minutes.

What did all this mean?

Her heart pounded in her chest. She had to know what was inside that chest. She decided to go to Mica and Ozul. They would know the most about the chest since it was in their village. Jumping to her feet, she hurried toward them. Their eyebrows met with concerned expressions as she approached them.

"Is something wrong, Sophia?" Mica asked.

She shook her head. "There is a strange chest in that hut over there," she pointed in the direction, "do you have any idea who it belongs to?"

Ozul and Mica exchanged confused glances before shaking their heads.

Ozul said, "That's been there for as long as I can remember. In fact, longer."

Sophia's shoulders slumped. Now what?

"If you can figure out a way to open it," Mica said, "then you can have whatever is in it."

"Good luck, though," Ozul said. "There have been quite a few that have tried. No one's been able to figure it out."

The difference between her and everyone else was that she had Ezekiel. And together they could open it. She knew it in her gut. If they couldn't get the chest opened, then there wouldn't be a force in the world that could.

She smiled. "I'll take you up on that. Thank you."

Both of the wraith brothers nodded and watched as she bounded off toward Ezekiel. He was still sitting with Andreas and Edric, laughing it up and having a good time. She slowed her pace, just to watch them. It filled her heart with joy to see them getting along still, acting like brothers.

Family.

That's what they all were. And she didn't want to rush in and take Ezekiel away, ending their fun moment. She stood next to him and waited for the story to be over. When all three of her men turned their attention to her, she smiled. "What's the joke?"

Andreas chuckled. "Just going over some of the stuff that happened in our past. Reliving the good stuff."

Sophia nodded. "Zeke, can I borrow you?"

"Sure." He climbed to his feet and dusted the back of his clothing off before facing her with a smile. "What are we doing?"

She smiled back. "You'll see."

He followed her back to the hut and when he stepped through, she pointed to the chest. "Think we can open it?"

His eyes widened and a spark of curiosity lit them, making the green glow brighter. "Damn right we can."

Sophia laughed. "Okay, let's get to it."

Ezekiel lowered himself in front of the chest and cupped his chin with his finger and thumb. His eyes narrowed on the numerous locks. He hummed to himself and hovered a hand over the chest. "Enchantments, traps. Yup. This one will be interesting."

"Interesting?" Sophia asked. "I've never heard of opening a chest being referred to as interesting."

He chuckled. "Be prepared for anything."

Taking out a piece of chalk, he started to write numerous symbols in an arc over the first lock and repeated the pattern for the remaining ones. After drawing a half circle over each and another symbol over the top, he laid his hand over them. The symbols started to glow and burn away as though they were never drawn to begin with. Clicks and grinding sounds came from the chest and a whooshing sound from the seal. A strange purple cloud seeped from within the chest and onto the ground. Ezekiel backed up and held an arm out in front of Sophia.

She peeked around his arm to watch a tiny, chubby creature with a long, pointed hat solidify in front of the chest. It hopped up to the top and pulled out a tiny sword and squeaked at them in an angry tone. The creature was unlike any Sophia had seen before. Still, Ezekiel didn't move. He seemed... cautious of the creature.

"Gnomes," he said. "Tricky little creatures."

"How harmful can they really be?" Sophia asked as she wanted to get closer. "As bad as the fairies?"

"Sometimes worse," Ezekiel said. "They are used to protecting things, like this chest. And they do so with their life. They have razor-sharp teeth and are vicious and quick."

"Great. So how do we open the chest then?" Sophia asked as the creature started to jump up and down, squeaking like mad and pointing its tiny sword at them. She stepped out from behind Ezekiel and faced the gnome. It took one look at her, made an 'ehr' noise, and lowered its sword.

"It's cute."

"It is a *he*, actually," Ezekiel said.

Sophia mused. "How can you tell?"

"The eyes." He shifted and she looked at him from over her shoulder. He seemed uncomfortable. She returned her gaze to the gnome. He sheathed his sword and took a seat on the chest. Sophia leaned closer and saw that the creature had eyes the color of amethysts.

"Hello," she said. "I like your eyes."

He returned soft squeaks and blushed.

Good. He could understand her. "I need to see what is in this chest. Would you let me do that, please?"

He squeaked and shook his head.

"I promise to return anything we don't need. I'm looking for the heirs to Nighthelm, and if there is something in this chest that can help," she pointed to it, "I will forever be grateful."

He seemed to think about it for a moment then shifted his gaze from Sophia to Ezekiel. He pointed and squeaked in quick succession, gesturing with his hands. She took it that he wouldn't let her in the chest until he left the room. She smiled and looked over her shoulder. "Would you mind leaving the hut for just a few minutes?"

His eyes grew wide and he gaped at her. "Fine. Just be careful."

She nodded and once he left, she faced the gnome again. "How about it, good sir? Can I see now?"

He hopped off the chest and sat next to Sophia. He yawned and closed his eyes. She smiled and opened the lid of the chest. Inside there were a number of trinkets and cloths. Under those were a map, scroll, and a diary. Sophia looked inside and couldn't make heads or tails of what the words said. It must have been in a different language.

She smiled. Good thing she had a sorcerer bookworm on her side. Closing the chest, she stood and quietly walked out of the hut.

~

SOPHIA

*E*zekiel was over the moon about the diary and map. He, Sophia, Edric, and Andreas spread the map on the floor of their hut and after studying it thoroughly, Edric and Ezekiel pointed out a location that was previously hidden and thought lost since the gods went to sleep.

Haris stomped around outside the hut. Sophia had released him to let him roam and get some exercise and to be in the woods he loved so much.

"Legend has it, nymph deities reside there," Ezekiel said, pointing to the location on the map.

"Nymphs?" Sophia asked.

He nodded. "They are demi-gods of the woods, and though lesser than the oracles, they are magical and timeless. Aware of so much more than man."

To hear him speak of them, it was like a precious gift and a dream come true for him. He ate this stuff up. Sophia thought she may never get over the child-like wonder he had with learning new things and jotting his observations down in his book.

"So, with the possibility of them still being there, I may be able to get some answers from them on the heirs," Sophia said.

"The question is would they share their knowledge? Not much is known about them beyond small paragraphs here and there. It was assumed they left the world or went into some sort of deep sleep along with the gods."

She hoped they would, and if they didn't, she would have to persuade them. Afterall, she was running out of options, and anything that could possibly lead her to the heirs was a clue worth following. "Any idea how to get there?"

Edric said, "It looks like the road there has been long overgrown. It would be a difficult trek, but we could probably make it there within a day."

"Hold on," Ezekiel said. He pointed to a part in the book. "According to this, the nymphs can be very distrusting of strangers, and secretive. Locating them may take some work. We may have to prove ourselves before they grant us permission to their secrets."

Andreas said, "Which probably means information on the heirs. And let's not forget that grimms live in those woods and are still very determined to kill her."

"We'll just have to take that risk," Sophia said. "I can't risk not following a potential clue to the heirs."

"And I can do some research and see how we can mask her scent to keep the grimms off us for as long as possible," Ezekiel said.

"Then it's settled," Edric said, wrapping up the map and handing it over to Ezekiel. "The only thing left to do is decide when to leave."

Ezekiel said, "I'll need two days to find materials and ingredients and prepare for masking our scent."

Sophia nodded. "Two days it is. Edric and Andreas, please set up the watch and inform those who need to know of the plan so that they are prepared to protect the village while we are gone. I'm going to go talk with

Haris and spend some time with him. He's not going to be happy about our decision."

"He's probably just getting weary of the constant danger," Andreas said. "I'm sure he would love some time with you. May help ease his mind."

She nodded. "He'll do anything to keep me safe. I think that's what worries him the most. My safety."

The men agreed, and she stood and went to find Haris while Ezekiel went to work on deciphering more of the map and getting prepared for keeping the grimms off their backs as much as possible.

CHAPTER THREE

EZEKIEL

*E*zekiel sat near the fire, scribbling down his findings regarding the map in his book. He heard a melodic laugh, and his attention was drawn to Sophia at the edge of the village, behind the huts, petting Haris as his head raised up and down repeatedly. He must have been excited about something she had told him, and his reaction caused her to laugh.

He sighed. That woman.

She filled a hole inside him, and he could never repay her for that with ten lifetimes.

Shaking his head, he returned to the map. It was enchanted previously. That much was for certain. He could still feel remnants of the magic that covered the paper, long faded, but still just enough for someone like him to detect it. However, it was a protection spell. Somehow, it must've been unlocked when

Sophia touched it. He closed his eyes and focused his energy on the paper. Every sorcerer had a "signature" with their spells. Though this one was at least ten years old, he could maybe pull enough of the energy to decipher who placed the spell to begin with. Maybe that would help Sophia with finding the heirs?

A pinch formed in his brow. There was enough of a trace to pick up the signature, just not from who. Releasing his focus, he opened his eyes. He couldn't figure out who cast the spell, and there was still a question of why. Why was there an enchantment in the first place? Not to mention being locked in an equally enchanted chest?

The far-right corner of the map was ripped where a remnant of an emblem of some sort or crest seemed to have been taken. Only the outer edges remained intact. Pulling out his notebook, he flipped to a clean page and jotted down the part of the emblem that was still visible. It wasn't much. Just the outline with a few interruptions. Still, it was a clue, and it was still a find. He would take notes more on the appearance of the crest, including who he felt it belonged to. Any clue was worth following, especially with a chest that was locked away, enchanted, and left in a wraith village.

Whoever hid the chest had done so to protect themselves and hide their identity. A crest wasn't just a mere artistic symbol, it represented a family and even one's ancestry and position in society. If someone purposefully obscured the crest, it was meant to conceal who they belonged to and where they came from. There had to be more to the findings within the chest, the map, and the diary. He knew there was more to this than what he could see at the moment, he just couldn't decide how.

He rolled up the map, tucking it away into his belongings, deciding to let that one be for a moment and took up the scroll in its place. This one was a detailed spell. One he hadn't seen before. His eyebrows drew together, and a pinch formed at the center of his forehead. The runes seemed rushed. Ink splattered the page, making some of the words nearly indecipherable, but not so much that Ezekiel couldn't figure them out.

There were a few words he could clearly pick out. Ones that belong to the goddesses. More referring to a phoenix, and some mentioning waking from a long sleep. He couldn't make the connection between the words he could easily decipher, but there was a tug in his gut that told him this scroll was somehow connected to the heirs. He couldn't tell how just yet. And his gut was rarely wrong.

CHAPTER FOUR

ANDREAS

*A*ndreas approached Edric and Ezekiel. Ezekiel's fingers scribbled away at the notes he was taking by the light of the fire, and he mumbled to himself. Andreas shook his head. "You know that book isn't going to talk back, right?"

Ezekiel looked up from his notes. His puzzled expression faded away to one of light-heartedness and fun. "Of course not. I'm not insane."

"Yet," Andreas said and laughed as he ducked out of the way of the book that Ezekiel threw at him.

"That's enough," Edric said. His voice was commanding and pulled Andreas's attention to him at once, but upon seeing the smile on the commander's face, Andreas relaxed the tension in his shoulders and smiled back. "We all know Ezekiel is sensitive about his books."

"What!" Ezekiel stood up and charged after Edric, colliding with his body at the waist. "I'll show you sensitive!"

Edric laughed while maintaining his foothold but took a few steps back. The laugh echoed through the village, causing a few concerned wraiths to step out and watch the fun. Andreas shook his head.

My brothers.

And they were. Because of Sophia. Though he could do with just a little less fighting in his life, he wouldn't change a thing about it. Sophia had brought them together and they had a family. Andreas didn't feel like he had to hide who he was with them. He felt at home. And that was one of the best feelings in the world.

Ezekiel pulled away and straightened his shirt. The biggest smile Andreas had ever seen on him stretched his lips.

Andreas held up his hands. "I only wanted to check in before I started my watch. Anything I need to know?"

Both Edric and Ezekiel shook their heads. Edric said, "It's been quiet."

"Yeah," Ezekiel said. "Almost too quiet."

"Let's not borrow trouble, shall we?" Andreas made his way toward the main entrance of the village. Halfway there, he turned and said, "You two don't have too much fun without me."

They waved him off and he chuckled as he took his post. He turned serious, watching every movement in the shadows. Darting from one to the next, he searched for any hint of someone waiting for the opportune moment to attack. The shadows were thick, and the woods were quiet. A few shifting bushes happened ever so often, but those were likely from any number of small game that lived in the Witch Woods. He shifted into his wraith form and rose up higher into the air to get a better look, just to make sure. A couple of jack rabbits rushed from one bush and into a burrow in the ground at the base of an old tree. He lowered himself to the ground and shifted back.

Nothing was there. Nothing threatening anyway.

As his eyes moved over the shadows, his mind recalled recent events. The attack from earlier was too close for comfort. Sophia only barely missed that arrow. He shook his head and let out a heavy breath. Damn it if he had to face a day with another possibility of her getting hurt. He couldn't stand to think of a hair on her head being harmed much less any bodily injuries. Murderous rage wouldn't come close to what he would fall into. Possibly destroy everything in his path.

She was capable, for sure. Held her own quite well. Always had. But there was always that one possibility. He couldn't let that come to pass.

She had completed him in more ways than one. Ever since she came into his life, she was his main focus. Despite having to share her, Sophia was *his* woman. If he was truthful with himself, he didn't even mind sharing her. He couldn't see any other men more suited for her than the two men he now considered brothers and shared Sophia's heart. He would likely raze the world for them as well. Not only would it hurt Sophia if something happened to them, it would hurt him too. He wouldn't give his family up for the world.

Family.

All because of Sophia and his newfound brothers, Edric and Ezekiel.

She was the glue that kept them together. He wished they could find the heirs soon, so they could live out their lives in relative peace, if that were a possibility for them. Though he felt like they were one step closer to finding the heirs, he doubted they would make it without more loss.

He just hoped that loss wouldn't be Edric, Ezekiel, or Sophia.

CHAPTER FIVE

SOPHIA

*S*ophia, Ezekiel, and Edric sat around a fire, enjoying their stew and each other's company. Ezekiel kept them entertained and laughing with interesting tales from his time training in the academy.

"I sat there thinking, what was the worst thing that could happen?" Ezekiel said as he described a spell that was supposed to change his appearance. "I set everything up, did the spell with a few substituted ingredients that were supposed to work in similar ways, and… POOF!"

He spread his fingers out wide and his eyes were animated. He took a deep breath and shrugged.

"I quickly found a mirror, and to my horror, I was green. A sickly, dingy, ugly green. My hair had fallen out in spots, and my nose was missing."

As her men laughed, Sophia joined in. The feeling was phenomenal. She hadn't laughed like this for as long as she could remember. Before her time with the men, Haris had seemed the only one that brought her joy. Now, she loved to laugh. She knew these moments were short lived, so taking in the chance to raucously laugh was too good to pass up. It also helped her to feel even closer to her men.

Mica and Ozul approached and inclined their heads to each of them in greeting. Ozul asked, "Want to see something really fun?"

Sophia exchanged glances with Edric and Ezekiel. They nodded. "What did you have in mind?" Sophia asked.

"Andreas, let's spar," Mica called out.

Andreas turned to face them from his perch on watch. His arms were crossed over his chest. He cocked an eyebrow and a slight smile pulled up one corner of his lips. He turned back around.

Mica and Ozul took turns egging him on. "Come on, brother, too scared to be showed up in front of your woman?" one said while the other laughed and said, "He's too tired."

Andreas turned around and started walking toward them. He made it halfway before he shifted to his wraith form and charged Mica, who shifted once he noticed that Andreas had.

Soon, wraiths filled the back half of the village while Mica and Andreas wrestled, waiting for their turn.

The sight was incredible, the blend of shadow and red glow, twisting in and out, pulling apart and then colliding together again. Sophia was in awe. She couldn't make heads or tails of who was who until they shifted back with Andreas on his feet and Mica on his back on the ground.

Andreas looked around and said, "Next?"

One by one, he continued to spar with them. Sophia was captivated as he won each round. The strength he gave her continued to pulse through her, and she couldn't seem to shake how powerful she felt just watching him wrestle with his fellow wraiths.

Andreas stood proud and tall, a big smile on his face as he turned around and said, "I'm just getting started. Who wants to take me on now?"

Edric stood and said, "I'll take both you and Zeke on at once!"

A rush of awe rustled through the crowd and Sophia sat back, watching. Ezekiel stood and said, "Just remember you asked for this," as he took Andreas's side.

Edric laughed. "Oh, I will remember. Remember how I beat the two of you. But don't worry. I'll remind you in case you forget."

The way the fire reflected off his smile sent an electric warmth through Sophia, hitting her hard in her core and wetness formed between her thighs.

They wrestled and it was like three men from opposite worlds were fighting it out for her hand, but all in fun. The show of the macho demonstration reminded her, with a man like Edric, she was completely untouchable, protected, and safe. He handled himself expertly, anticipating each move as though he had lived this scenario hundreds of times. Like how he dodged a blow from Ezekiel while knocking down Andreas, and still managing not to lose a beat. He rolled on the ground, climbed to his feet in one smooth motion, and avoided the kick from Andreas.

Edric laughed. "Come on! You can do better than that!"

Andreas rushed to her, picking her up from the ground and pulling her to his and Ezekiel's side. Sophia smiled coyly and kicked Andreas's legs from under him then spun to face Ezekiel. His eyes grew wide and he gulped as she stood her ground, facing off with him. Edric made a move to stand by her, and she made a single step backward and kicked him in his back, sending him to the ground.

She laughed.

"I thought you were on my side," Edric said as he stood and dusted himself off.

"I saved her," Andreas said.

"No, you didn't," Sophia said, and they took turns sparring with each other. She couldn't stop smiling to save her soul, and she knew that gave some of her moves away. No matter what she did, she couldn't become as serious as they were, though she could see the love in each of their eyes.

She knew she could never live a day without any of them. And not just because they each held a piece of her soul, which she was glad for, but because they truly completed her. Each of them added a piece to her life she was missing, and she was ever grateful to have them with her.

Despite the search for the heirs and the constant danger nipping at their heels, it was nice to take a break and just relax and have fun with her men. She was having so much fun, that when it came time to switch watch, she was saddened.

Edric walked with Sophia to the entrance of the village. He said, "Don't worry, my love. We will have more days like this. Without the constant worry of a fight."

"Hopefully soon," she said and smiled. "That was so much fun. Felt like it ended too soon."

He nodded. "Soon."

"Do you think we are close to finding the heirs?" Sophia asked.

He shrugged. "It's very possible. If anyone can do it, I know it's you."

She smiled. "I appreciate your faith in me."

"It's well deserved," Edric said and pulled her into him to kiss her on the forehead.

She sighed. "Sometimes I wonder if I don't bring more danger to your lives than good. Take the mountain for example."

"We survived. Albeit through some rather close calls, but you have to look at the good. We found that girl. We don't know who she is or why she is locked in the crystal coffin, but she could be important. Maybe even imperative to your hunt for the heirs."

"True, but—"

"And we freed a bunch of people who were probably closer to death than anyone cares to admit, which gained some pretty amazing friends."

"Again, you're right," Sophia said. "About the girl, though. We still need to find a way to wake her up, and I would love the chance to talk to Zeke about his findings of the map and scroll. I just can't risk being exhausted in case of another attack."

"Fair point," he said. "You should let us take on some of the work though. You don't have to do it all on your own. We are here to help you."

Sophia grinned. "You all are incredible. I'm grateful for all that you do. I couldn't ask you to take on more than you already have."

"That's what we are here for. To help you in your journey, fight with and for you. Let us do that," Edric said, his voice was soft and kind, soothing.

She looked at her arm and decided to free Haris so he could roam. "*Vocavi.*"

His green mist floated from her arm, dissolving the image, and solidifying in front of her. He nudged her in thanks before disappearing into the woods without being seen by the others. He trilled in the distance. Sophia smiled.

Her mind became preoccupied with the possibility of being closer than ever to finding the heirs and hoping beyond all hope that this wasn't just another dead end.

"What can I do to help your mind?" Edric asked.

She looked at him with a puzzled expression.

He chuckled. "I can see the gears turning in your head."

"Do you think the nymphs will help us?" Sophia asked.

"Won't know unless we try," he said. "We'll leave and make our way toward the location on the map. From there, all we can do is ask. For now, let's focus on resting so we can be prepared for anything that comes our way."

She smiled again and the tension in her shoulders relaxed a little. She loved how protected and safe she felt when with Edric. How not even a care in the world could ever affect her. Even the what-ifs that tore at her mind.

*E*dric watched Sophia as she slept a little before joining his brothers, Andreas and Ezekiel. They stood watch at the entrance of the village and seemed very involved in their conversation. Ezekiel motioned with his hands and his face was animated.

"What did you say to get him started?" Edric asked Andreas. "You'll never get him to stop now."

Andreas chuckled while Ezekiel fake-punched him in the arm. "I'll have you know," he said, "we were discussing the scroll and the emblem on the map from the chest."

Edric nodded and glanced back at the hut where Sophia slept. He turned his gaze back to Andreas and Ezekiel. "What did you find out?"

Andreas shook his head. "That's just it. According to Zeke, it seems like it was intentionally removed."

Edric frowned. "Where is it?"

Ezekiel pulled the map from his satchel hanging against his waist and handed it to Edric. He unrolled it and stared at the torn righthand corner. Musing to himself, he held it closer to the light of a nearby torch. While he studied the outline features, Ezekiel said, "The chest had a crest as well, but it was of a phoenix. The outline of that crest doesn't come anywhere close to matching."

Edric nodded, rolled up the map, and handed it back to Ezekiel. "I believe it is the crest of the Averells. That was a symbol of a crowned griffon. If you look closely on the edges, you can see a tip of a hind leg and the end of the tail."

Ezekiel's eyebrows drew together, and he unrolled the map to take a closer look at the remnants of the symbol. "Yes. I see it."

"Question is," Andreas said, "Why hide it in a chest in the middle of a wraith village? I can't think of any kingdom or family crest that has a phoenix. They certainly aren't wraith."

Edric asked, "What did the scroll say?"

Ezekiel sighed as he rolled the map up again and tucked it into his satchel. "I have yet to decipher it. It is made to look like an enchantment, but the runes were rushed. There are a few references I could make out, but nothing to lead me to exactly what sort of enchantment it is yet."

Edric nodded. "I suspect that the recent attacks have something to do with Sophia and the heirs."

"Do you think there will be another attack from those assassins from the mountain?" Andreas asked.

Edric shrugged. "It is a possibility we need to be prepared for. We also need to keep a look out for the Nighthelm guard. They know we came into the woods and despite the rumors regarding the dangers of traveling into them at night, I wouldn't put it past them to try."

"I believe the assassins were sent by whoever remained loyal to Lady Naomi," Ezekiel said. "However, it could be that the Blood Queen had returned and is trying to dispatch of any threats. Because Sophia killed Lady Naomi, the Blood Queen may see her as a threat."

"Agreed," Edric said. "The attack wasn't random. We should reinforce our defenses, especially before we leave."

Ezekiel nodded. "I'll reinforce the traps around the perimeter of the camp."

Andreas said, "And I will set up random treks around those traps with my wraith brothers. If there are any signs of danger, it will help us better prepare for the next attack."

"Sounds solid," Edric said.

Ezekiel left to prepare for the traps and Andreas went to send out a perimeter check. Edric was left to his own thoughts and the soft whisperings of the Witch Woods. As soon as the sky started to lighten, a sensation came over Edric. A sense of impending danger. His nerves burned like fire as his eyes raked through the shadows of the Witch Woods. Nothing seemed out of place. And there wasn't any movement. But that feeling didn't decrease. It only increased.

Something was there, and whatever it was, it was clever enough to remain hidden.

Haris approached and stomped his foot, sounding rather displeased instead of his happy little trills.

"Get Sophia," Edric whispered to Haris.

He nodded his large head, antlers catching the light of the rising sun, and rushed off through the woods.

Edric looked at Andreas and Ezekiel as they returned. They were on edge as well, eyes focused on the woods and shoulders tensed.

Good.

They felt the same thing he did.

A loud howl erupted through the woods. Grimms shifted from the shadows, approaching the outline of the camp, moving about as though they stalked prey. But they stopped just outside of the traps Ezekiel had laid. Either they knew the traps were there, or they were smart enough not to approach a platoon's worth of wraiths. Either way, they stood, glaring at him and his brothers.

As Sophia stepped up behind Edric, one of the grimms shifted.

"Her. She hurt us. Give her to us," the biggest grimm said. The voice forced goosebumps to run down Edric's arm. But he shoved that feeling away. They wanted Sophia. And there was no way he was going to give her over without a fight. Not even then.

She stepped forward, holding her sword and dagger at the ready. She was fierce and ready to fight despite just waking up. Edric was in awe of her and her ability to stand tall and battle ready the way she did.

"You. Why do you have sword of the great kings?" The grimm shifted to the side. "You are thief!"

The blades started to glow, and the more they glowed, the more powerful she looked. Edric wondered if the magic was channeled through the weapons as well, giving her additional control and strength. Even before, she was a force to reckon with. The way she looked, she was even more so now.

"Answer us," the grimm commanded.

Edric stepped forward, angered and ready to die for her. They had been after his woman since before they met, and he would rather die for her than risk her being injured by those revenge-bent creatures. "You will have to go through me before you even get close to her."

"No. We want her. Not you," the raspy terrifying voice held a hint of anger. "We won't leave. Not until she is ours."

"You'll be waiting a long time," Andreas said. He shifted into his wraith form. Edric looked behind him, finding rows of wraiths floating like deadly, black forms with glowing red eyes.

He knew the grimms were stalling, but not why. They didn't seem the kind to be afraid of a challenge much less the size of the army they had. And how they managed to stay outside of the traps. Self-preservation was never a concept he figured the grimms had. There had to be more to their appearance than demanding Sophia.

"I'm not leaving," Sophia said, holding her head high. "And I'm not a thief."

"You owe us!" the grimm said, pacing a few steps in each direction, managing to keep its wolf-like head focused on Sophia.

"Never," she said, voice echoing through the woods.

Something caught the grimms' attention as they all simultaneously turned their attention in the same direction. Then, all at once, they left without another word.

Edric shifted his attention to Sophia who gaped at

the empty woods and shook her head, sheathing her weapons.

"That was rather underwhelming," Edric said.

"You said it," Sophia said. "Doesn't make sense though."

"No, it doesn't," Ezekiel said. There was something in his voice Edric couldn't quite place. He looked to the sorcerer, finding a puzzled, almost angry look on his face.

Andreas said, "It was probably a tactic to throw us off guard because they managed to avoid the traps. Seemed like they did so with great effort."

"Which isn't fair. Not a single one so much as stepped a paw on a trap. I have captured countless creatures in my traps. They've never failed."

Edric chuckled, "You're getting rusty and need more practice."

"Too much reading, not enough doing?" Andreas asked.

Ezekiel turned red in the face, fists clenched at his sides.

Edric and Andreas nodded and clapped Ezekiel on the back at the same time.

"Cheer up," Edric said. "You'll get them next time."

Andreas said, "Besides, we were only teasing you. It's so easy to do. And fun."

"Still," Ezekiel muttered.

"I think it's safe to say we all agree that the grimms

avoiding the traps is odd," Edric said as they moved toward the cooking fire.

Despite nodding and seemingly improving in his mood, Ezekiel still muttered something about adding another perimeter of traps just to be on the safe side. Edric watched as he walked out of the village and wondered if it wasn't just an added measure for safety but to soothe the wounded ego a bit.

Shaking that thought aside, he turned to Andreas and asked, "Have the wraiths returned from patrol yet?"

Andreas's eyebrows pulled together. "No. They haven't. They should've been back by now."

On cue, the wraiths showed up. Andreas greeted them and asked, "You missed out on quite the show. Have you seen or heard anything while out? What took so long?"

They all exchanged confused glances, and the one in front said, "We did only as you suggested. We did the perimeter and came back. We saw nor heard anything."

Andreas gave them a curt nod and dismissed them. Though he seemed even more puzzled by what he learned. Edric asked him about that.

Andreas said, "Nothing about this makes any sense."

"I agree," Edric said.

"Wraiths are excellent trackers. They would've

heard that howl. With how close we are to Nighthelm, I'm guessing some of the guard even heard it. Which begs the question of why they were so close to the city to begin with."

"So, did they show up, or were they sent?" Edric asked.

"Well if you figure it out, be sure to let me know. I'm going to get some sleep."

Edric nodded and watched as he walked off.

CHAPTER SEVEN

SOPHIA

*S*ophia twirled the dagger in her hand as she sat near the cooking fire. She stared at a spot on the ground. The words the grimms had said to her replayed through her mind.

What did they mean by thief? How could she be a thief if she was given the weapons as gifts?

Nothing of the word "thief" made any sense to her, and she wondered what made the grimms think she stole them. She shifted her attention to the sword that glowed with her every touch and wondered if there was more to the gifts that Grindel and the oracles gave her than what she originally thought.

In an effort to connect the dots, she came up with a whole lot of nothing.

The sword was a gift from the oracles, to help her

find the heirs. But the dagger? That was just an expensive birthday gift from Grindel. But it also glowed with her hands as well.

The gifts puzzled her. Despite her confusion, she knew deep down that it was a sign of her destiny to find the heirs and restore them to the throne.

Sitting around and waiting for them to fall into her lap wasn't going to happen. She stood from the ground, sheathed her dagger, and helped out with refortifying the village.

Within a few hours, she met up with her men. "Is everything ready?" she asked.

Edric nodded. "I believe the village will be safe while we are gone."

"I've added even more traps around the perimeter. Nothing is going to be able to get close enough to the village and not trip them off," Ezekiel said. "I'm ready to administer the scent blocker."

Sophia nodded. Ezekiel sprayed her first. Next was Edric, and Andreas. Finally, himself.

Andreas smiled and said, "Doesn't smell that bad. Let's get this show on the road."

They turned and left the village while Ezekiel studied the map and directed them on where to go. Haris joined them once they were out of sight of the village. Sophia smiled and pet his flank. He trilled and bumped into her, almost knocking her over. She chuckled.

There was a cracking sound, like a branch breaking under too much weight. The group fell silent, stopping for a few moments to search the woods. Even during the day, when the sun was directly above them, the shadows were thick. Not a lot of light showed between the trees. The darkness of Witch Woods was impenetrable. Only ever so often did a few of the sun's rays ever peek through the thick canopy of trees. And even then, it wasn't enough to keep the dark at bay.

They continued on their journey, constantly searching the shadows for even the slightest movement. Even Haris seemed on edge. She couldn't stand that her friend was so uncomfortable. She patted him on his flank again, to let him know everything would be okay.

He nudged her as a rumbling sound came from his throat. He pranced a few steps, shaking his head from side to side. He nearly hit Andreas with his antlers. Andreas laughed and rubbed his hand along Haris's snout.

"Careful, boy," Andreas said.

Haris trilled.

"Seems like even he is growing weary of the constant tension," Ezekiel said.

Edric said, "It can't last forever."

It wouldn't. She was certain of it. All Sophia could do was try her best and take it day-by-day. And having Haris accompany them, hamming things up in his typical yakshi way, it was a nice break from the constant threat of danger. They had each other to lean on, they would be all right.

CHAPTER EIGHT

SOPHIA

*I*t was late in the evening when they came to a clearing marked by a stone wall that barely reached the midpoint on Sophia's thigh. It was circular, and a single archway led into the area. In the center, bordered by glowing rocks weaving between them, was a copse of trees. Around them were butterflies that held a soft purple glow. Even some of the bushes shed a soft aura. However, the trees themselves seemed ordinary. Just regular trees that found their home in Witch Woods.

Sophia wasn't sure about what stood in front of her. It could be a trap. Or, it could work out in their favor. Either way, Sophia called Haris back to her arm before she cautiously stepped forward, entering the small enclosure. She heard her men shuffle behind her. Holding up her hand, she signaled for them to wait and continued forward.

Rustling came from the bushes. Sophia halted mid-step. She held her breath as her eyes darted from tree to tree and shadow to shadow.

"Why do you wake us, Little Bird?" There was more than one voice, speaking as one. It sounded magical, terrifying, and yet beautiful all at once.

Sophia narrowed her eyes on the shadows and said, "I seek answers."

"Answers to what?" they asked.

Sophia sighed. *Here goes nothing.* "I'm looking for the heirs of Nighthelm, so that they may reclaim the throne."

The voices said, "We may have the answers you seek, but you must first complete a task."

Of course. With her luck, she would be forced to dance blindfolded around a firepit amidst the vengeful grimms.

Sophia sighed. "What do I have to do?"

Four figures emerged from within the trees. At first, their skin matched the tress, but the bark smoothed away to reveal rich browns, greys, and even white. They were women, standing stark naked with long flowing black hair and glowing, hazel colored eyes.

When they spoke, their mouths didn't move. Yet

their words surrounded Sophia, as though they were carried on the wind. "Touch the heart."

They gestured to a tree in the center of the copse that shifted and revealed a glowing, teal colored heart.

She looked over her shoulder at her men. They shook their heads. None of them looked too thrilled about what the nymphs asked her to do. Edric's hands rested on the hilt of his sword. She slightly shook her head. He hesitated for a brief moment but released his sword. Comforted by that sight, she continued toward the tree. As she drew closer, a strange drumming hum surrounded her. She felt the pull of magic lure her closer.

This had better not be a trap.

She reached out a hand toward the heart. Her fingers brushed against the surface. It glowed brighter, enveloping her in the bluish-green light. The brightness increased, stabbing at her eyes and her mind.

Just when she couldn't take the pain any longer, the light receded. Panting for breath, fighting against a wave of nausea, she peeled her eyes open to find she was no longer standing in Witch Woods, next to the nymphs, but in front of a tree hovering high above the clouds. Roots entangled a circular piece of earth. Orbs of different colored lights, bright pinks, blues, purples, and white swirled around her.

Where the fuck am I?

She had no idea what would happen when she

touched the stone. Certainly not this. She had somehow been transported, and now stood who knew where. The sun nestled against the horizon of cloud, shining brighter than she had ever seen. The sky was a vibrant blue.

As beautiful as the scene was, she didn't know how to get back. And that was a problem.

"Choose an orb," the voices said.

Sophia turned around and looked at the orbs as one of each color hovered in front of her. Each one held a different symbol.

"What are they?" she asked.

"Your trial." The voices said, soft and sweet. Never mind that the last time she faced a "trial" she ended up in the mountain and nearly watched two of her men be sucked dry from the poisonous magic.

"What sort of trial?" Sophia asked.

"Each orb contains a possible outcome of your life," the nymphs said. "Choose wisely, for it will sway our decision to help you."

"So, this is a test?" she asked.

No answer.

Perfect.

Everything had to be so damned cryptic. None of what they offered helped her to know which orb was which. She stared at each of them. She knew she couldn't take forever making a decision. They all looked inviting. But she couldn't pick all of them. Just one.

Closing her eyes, she extended her hand and touched one. There was another pull and she was lifted and swimming through air, as magic swirled around her. She kept her eyes closed, waiting for the sensation to stop. When it did, she opened her eyes.

She was in a cabin. A nice one. Fancy furnishings covered nearly every inch of the floor and she smiled at the familiar feeling. She knew this place. This was home. Though she didn't know how she knew that, it was something that resonated with her. Memories floated through her mind of things that had yet to pass, and she mused over the peacefulness that surrounded her.

She walked to the door and pulled it open. Woods, bathed in the orange-red glow of sunset, stood in front of her. Not too far off was the sound of an ocean, and she could smell the salty sea as the wind blew into her.

Edric approached from behind her, wrapping her in his arms and warmth. He rested his chin on her shoulder and left a kiss on her cheek.

Just as she wondered where Andreas and Ezekiel were, she saw them. Andreas floated through the trees, freely, in his wraith form, while the sound of chopping wood came from the side of the house. Ezekiel walked around front, joining Sophia and Edric at the door as Andreas shifted to his human form and approached.

She smiled at her men. They looked so happy and healthy. Her heart warmed being near them, and she wanted to lie on the grass to watch the sky, picking out shapes in the clouds. She nearly laughed at herself for such thoughts. She wasn't like the other girls in Nighthelm that swooned over the silliest romantic notion. But the peace here offered her a freedom she had never known before.

Though she didn't know how, she knew that they could breathe without the threat of her living with a broken soul, without worry of an attack from one creature or another, from standing guard and always fighting.

It was a dream. And though this place felt so real, she knew it was only an illusion. But this place held such an allure. Sophia wondered if this was something she could really have. Peace and love. With her men at her side.

"We can make that happen for you," the nymphs said. "All you have to do is ask."

Could she?

Nighthelm needed her, even though the people would never admit to needing an *anima contritum* like her. Andreas pulled on her hand, dragging her from Edric's loving embrace, and led her through the woods on the other side of the cabin, closer to the sound of the ocean. As soon as they stepped through the break in the woods, Sophia's eyes focused on the jade colored ocean against the light navy blue of the evening sky.

Her breath stilled for a moment.

There was such beauty in this little paradise of theirs. So much wonder and awe.

All you have to do is ask... the nymphs' words repeated through her mind like a distant, echoing whisper.

"Stay with us," Andreas said, pulling Sophia's attention to him. Edric and Ezekiel flanked him.

She smiled. But words failed her. She loved her men. Truly, and as much as she wanted to stay with them in this magical place, this paradise, she knew she couldn't. But there was so much weight and longing in knowing all she had to do was reach out to them, touch them, let them hold her. No more running. No more fighting.

The nymphs' words echoed again.

Edric held out his hand. "Please, stay."

This wasn't real. But she so wanted it to be. And though she knew all she had to do was ask, she couldn't. Nighthelm needed her.

Settling her gaze on each of her men, she said, "I can't."

She rushed back to the cabin.

The nymphs' voices surrounded her again. "We can

make this real. No one will ever find you here. No one would ever bother you again. Peace and love forever…"

"I can't. Not when Nighthelm needs me."

"What is your decision then?"

"I choose to fight. To do what is right. I choose justice." Sophia spun in circles as the world started to blur and run like water down a windowpane. "My men chose me. They chose my fight. They will be with me through it all."

"Even if they die in the process?"

Sophia squared her shoulders and stood firm. "I won't let that happen."

"But you can't—"

"I won't let that happen," she said, hands clenched at her sides. "I would die for them, happily. For Nighthelm. I won't abandon the people who need me most."

The cabin and everything around her faded to black. Sophia focused on her breaths as the magic that brought her to this place surrounded her once more. The emotion in her still felt real. The things she saw felt real. But it was only an illusion. A test.

Magic tugged on her. A sinking feeling entered her gut. She closed her eyes and let the magic take her back to the tree with the glowing "heart."

~

SOPHIA

*W*hen Sophia opened her eyes, she was back inside the copse of trees, surrounded by the nymphs in the Witch Woods. Her men stood behind her, appearing relieved that she was there. She shifted her gaze back to the nymphs and felt anger burn within her. She was forced to make a decision she never wanted to make.

They smiled at her.

"Will you answer my questions or not, now?" she asked, voice sharp.

The all lowered their heads. Sophia hoped that meant yes.

"I'm looking for—"

"The heirs of Nighthelm," the nymphs said. "One is no longer. But the other lies in wait, between worlds. Healing. Frozen in time."

Great. More riddles. Although Sophia instantly thought of the girl in the crystal coffin. She didn't bring it up though. She was still unsure of who to trust with that information. She wanted no one but herself and her men to know of the girl and her location—and that included Nymphs. What they had just forced her through did little to encourage her faith in them. Still, what they offered was a solid lead to go by. She decided to wait until she could talk to her men about her suspicion and discuss plans then.

"Take heed, Guardian. The heir must awaken by the next full moon. If not, the heir will pass on."

Sophia narrowed her eyes and a pinch formed in her brow. "What do you mean by pass on? Do you mean die?"

"Yes. The magic that protects the heir grows weaker by the day."

"What can I do to stop it?" Sophia asked.

The nymphs drew closer to their trees, and their forms began to shift back to the color of the bark. "Your dagger and sword are the keys to your success. Even your forest spirit can help you restore the heir. But be warned, Little Bird. There are dangers even we cannot see that block your path."

Their eerie voices became softer, more distant. Sophia shook her head. She already knew the things they had just said. She was growing more frustrated with riddle after riddle. She needed a solid direction in which to go.

"Return to the heirs' beginning, young one. Your answer lies there…"

They disappeared into their trees and the copse fell silent and cold.

Sophia stared at the trees. She wasn't done asking questions yet. She still wanted to know why they would force her to make a decision like that. After several moments of staring with her hands tightly balled into fists at her sides, she let out a heavy breath and turned to face her men.

"I take it you heard all of that?" she asked.

They nodded. Ezekiel said, "It sounds like we have to head back to Nighthelm. Again."

"I agree," Edric said. "That is where the heirs began."

Sophia nodded. Time was of the essence. There was no telling who else might have been looking for the heir as well. She felt like she was running out of time. She knew there was danger. Though whoever was behind the disappearance of the heirs succeeded in killing one, the other was still alive. And she had until the next full moon, which was in less than two weeks.

Determination renewed her faith and hope. She had to find the heir before someone else did. She would be damned if the last heir died before she had a chance to bring peace to Nighthelm.

"Let's head back to the village. We have a trip to plan," she said, and the men followed her out of the strange home of the nymphs.

CHAPTER NINE

SOPHIA

*S*ophia sat in the hut, staring at the sword lying in her lap. The words the nymphs had told her swirled through her mind, and she was further away from solving the problem.

Go back to the heirs' beginning...

Well at least that part was easy. Nighthelm. The problem was how would they get in? The castle blocked their attempts and the entire Nighthelm army was on alert for her and her men. They were seen as enemies of the city. And she was seen as an *anima contrium*. It was kill first and ask questions later for her kind. Never mind the risk to her men. She couldn't allow harm to come to them. There had to be a better way into Nighthelm.

The dagger and sword are your keys to success...

What sort of power did the sword hold? She

couldn't deny how much stronger and more in control she felt when she wielded the weapon. But using it just seemed wrong since it was meant for the heirs—well, heir—and not her.

Andreas took a seat next to her. He gently bumped her with his shoulder. She met his gaze and there was hope, love, and everything she could possibly imagine lighting up his eyes. He said, "What troubles you so much?"

She wanted to tell him all about what she saw. About the nymphs offering a life of peace and serenity. No more fighting and no more constant brushes with death. She wanted to tell them how real it felt and how badly she wanted to say yes. She would do anything to protect them, even if it came at a price. But for now, she will keep fighting It wasn't a decision made lightly, and she certainly hoped she would be able to share in that life when she finally fulfilled her destiny.

She sighed. "I can't figure out how to find the heir if we can't get into Nighthelm to do what the nymphs told me to."

He nodded. "Well, that is a challenge. But not an impossible one."

Ezekiel said, "Andreas is right. We still have yet to check the archives under the castle."

"True," Sophia said. "But how do we get in there?"

Edric shifted. "There are many hidden doors

within the walls. It's possible one of them will lead to the archives."

"Yes," Andreas added with a smile. "See? We can work through anything together."

Sophia grinned. "What about the sword? The nymphs said the dagger and sword were my keys to success."

"The sword is likely just a means to an end," Edric said.

Ezekiel added, "One we haven't tried yet."

"Well," Sophia said as she settled her gaze on each of her men, "the only thing left to do is to go try."

The men agreed.

"We should leave under the cover of night. It will be much easier to get in than during the day," Edric said.

"And less dangerous," Andreas added.

"We can't wait long," Ezekiel said. "The nymphs said something about the next full moon. I highly suggest we do this tomorrow evening."

"Agreed." Sophia felt much better having talked with her men about her troubles. She smiled, loving them all the more. They made the problem easy to handle. She appreciated that.

Ezekiel stood. "I'm going to study the items from the chest more. I have a feeling there is a further link to the heir than what lay on the surface."

"Andreas and I have watch," Edric said.

"That means you should get some rest," Andreas said and followed Edric out of the hut.

Though she didn't feel tired, she knew she needed all the rest she could get. She lay down and closed her eyes and waited for sleep to take her.

CHAPTER TEN

EZEKIEL

*E*zekiel paused in his notes. He couldn't believe what he saw. After double checking his work, he had discovered he was wrong. So very, very wrong.

After trying his best to copy the runes in his notebook, he found a pattern. Most spells were cryptic to a point, but never with a pattern like this. It was subtle but stood out to him. Any other regular sorcerer would've paid the nonsense no mind and tossed the scroll into a fire. But not him.

The scroll wasn't a spell. It was a page quickly scrawled in code to appear like a spell so that whoever was protecting the heirs could do so without anyone else finding out.

For example, instead of a rune that looked like an upward pointed arrow, it was a wide "W". There were even instances with a rune in the shape of an "F" with the arms pointed downward instead of bending upward in the middle. Those subtle little changes would escape a less skilled sorcerer. He took those instances and rewrote them in his notebook. It spelled out Ripthorn.

Excitement burst inside him. He could hardly contain himself. His new findings were epic and definitely helpful. Replacing his items into his satchel, he stood and rushed to Edric and Andreas.

"You won't believe what I just discovered," Ezekiel said.

Andreas made a jab about something to do with some bookish spell to change his hair color, but Ezekiel ignored him.

"It's a coded note for whoever was charged with protecting the heirs. The map points to a secret passage within the castle walls that was designed for the heirs to leave. That was the location where the protector was supposed to meet the heirs and take them to safety."

Edric crossed his arms over his chest and said, "But something went wrong. One heir died."

"Exactly! And the other is still missing... you were there. You know what the nymphs said. But the clue they gave us was to return to the heirs' beginning." He held up the map and the scroll. "That means

Nighthelm. And the last place we have a chance to look is within the archives."

Edric nodded. "During my time as commander, I was privy to certain passages and backways for emergency purposes. I know where guards would be located. With this map, we can avoid those locations. We get in using that location, find the archives, get the information—especially the heirs' names, and figure out which one is still alive."

Andreas moved in closer and said, "We can find the heir, restore him to the throne, and get the pardon we so very much need."

Ezekiel nodded. "With this scroll and map at our side, we can find out what happened to the last heir."

"Excellent," Edric said, slapping a hand over Ezekiel's shoulders. "We have a plan."

"When do we tell Sophia?" Andreas asked.

"When she wakes up," Edric said. "She needs the rest."

The men agreed. Ezekiel returned to the hut and decided to get some rest himself. If he could stave off the excitement long enough to get tired.

CHAPTER ELEVEN

SOPHIA

*S*ophia couldn't sleep.

She wasn't alone though. Andreas kept her company, and made her feel stronger, but her worry kept sleep at bay. Edric and Ezekiel were finalizing plans for the run into Nighthelm later that evening.

His strong arms helped to ease the chaos within her, but her mind was flooded with finding the last heir before the next full moon, and she also couldn't get that test from the nymphs out of her mind. It was so tempting to say "yes" to their offer of peace, to blissfully stay in that other world. However, the more she thought on it, the more she realized that they were testing whether she was the type of person to choose what was right over what was easy.

She chose what was right. And she wanted to keep

her men safe. She refused to let anything happen to them.

Regardless of her feelings toward the test, she still needed to find the last heir. She thought over the riddle the oracles gave her, what the nymphs told her, and how the grimms called her a thief. All the while, that girl in the crystal coffin they found in the mountain stayed at the forefront of her mind. The image of her was as though Sophia stood next to the coffin even though she was far from the mountain cave they had found her in.

"Can't sleep?" Andreas asked.

She shook her head and let out a heavy sigh.

"Wanna talk about it?" He pulled her in closer.

She curled into his embrace and relished in the warmth of his body pressed against hers. "I just can't stop thinking of the girl in the coffin. I know she is somehow tied into this. The how is what eludes me."

"What makes you think she is related to you finding the heir?" he asked, warm breath tracing down her neck.

The sensation created a bit of pressure between her thighs, and she tried her best to clench them to ease the ache a little. "That's just it. I'm not sure."

"If it makes you feel any better, the archives hold the secrets of the royals. We are bound to find something solid there. And then we can worry about the girl. One step at a time, love." He rubbed his hand along her arm, and he pressed a kiss on her temple. "For now, you should rest."

She appreciated his attempt to comfort her, but it was doing little else than awakening need within her body.

"You have the sword of the kings to help you. You have us men to stand behind you. Nothing is going to stand in your way. I won't allow it." His lips gently brushed her ear lobes and warm tingles rippled through her nerves. That pressure between her thighs increased and was accompanied by a delicious warmth.

She smiled at his words and said, "I still don't like the idea of using a weapon meant for the heir. But if it is the only way I can find the heir, then so be it."

Still, there was a connection between it all that she wasn't able to make, and that threatened to send her mind reeling once more. She knew she needed the rest, but she also desperately needed to make that connection.

"Sleep on it, love. We'll tackle this once you've gotten some rest." His voice was so alluring. And convincing.

He was right though. She wouldn't be useful to anyone sleep-deprived. She rolled to face him, wrapping her arms around him and hitching a leg over his. She closed her eyes and waited for sleep to claim her, but damn it if her body didn't hum with Andreas's nearness.

Angling her head, she pressed her lips to his, kissing him deeply. She needed his comfort and his touch. She wanted more of that feeling he gave her that made her stronger and more powerful. Never mind the release of her built up tension would be an added benefit.

Andreas responded with fiercer kissing, his arms fumbling with the lace of her shirt. She felt his need building through his pants against hers. She softly moaned as she worked his shirt over his head.

Once they were freed of the constricting clothing, Sophia's back lay against the fur blanket, the tiny hairs tickling her skin, creating goosebumps along her arms as Andreas kissed along her belly up to her chest and her neck, finally ending with her lips. He slowly entered her, thrusting in a gentle rhythm. Giving her comfort and further relaxing her.

She loved that he was being selfless in his lovemaking, even appreciated that he wanted to help comfort her as well as please her, and that made her happy. It was freeing, especially since she had lived most of her life relatively alone. She never thought she would be given the chance to share a moment like this with him or anyone else. To have this was a gift that she would forever appreciate.

His gentle movements were filled with passion. He

was very attentive, which she adored. She moved with him, aiding in the crest of her release. And as she reached the apex of her climax, she felt relaxed, and her nerves were eased.

He laid next to her, scooping her into his arms and holding her as sleep came. A gentle kiss on her forehead was the last thing she was aware of before a deep, dreamless slumber.

～

SOPHIA

*A*s the last light of day trickled away, Sophia peeled her eyes open. She left the bed and stretched, feeling renewed and refreshed. After quickly dressing, she joined her men finishing up the preparations to leave for another attempt at getting into Nighthelm.

Her body buzzed with energy and her mind went full-tilt on the possibilities of finding another clue. She hoped that clue wouldn't lead to a dead end, but she had to try.

The men greeted her with a smile and a nod as they packed up supplies. Ezekiel approached her with an impish smile. "I have some news for you."

"I hope it is good news, judging by that smile of

yours," she said, a trace of a chuckle vibrated through her words.

He nodded. "I've decoded the scroll. It's directions to a secret location intended to get the heirs to safety. Though it didn't work out exactly according to plan, Edric and I correlated it with the map and we found a way into the archives with hopefully little resistance."

"Excellent," she said. That gave her hope that they weren't following a dead end.

"We will likely need the sword to unlock the door," he said.

She nodded, hoping the sword would do the trick.

She was ready more than ever to finally find a solid lead that would help her restore the heir to the throne. She just hoped it wouldn't be too late.

Everything was set. The men were ready. She led them back into the Witch Woods.

The trek seemed too quiet. It was a type of quiet that caused Sophia's nerves to be set on alert. Her gaze darted between shadows, and she knew there was something within the dark recesses that watched them.

Her men were silent as they walked with her, moving as quietly as ghosts. None of them seemed to want to make a sound for fear that whatever watched them would stalk them to the castle and lurch forward and attack.

But maybe that was better than leading some

horrific monster into the castle's walls. Sophia didn't know. Many of the creatures in Witch Woods were dangerous, sure. But most of them were very much so misunderstood.

A creak and pop sounded off to the left while crunching leaves echoed from the right. Sophia pulled on her sword. She knew from the sounds around them that they weren't just being watched, they were being stalked. Only a few creatures did this. Minotaurs and grimms. Neither were particularly on her list of things to bump into, much less fight.

She looked to her men and saw that they each held weapons of their own, aimed and ready. She nodded at them. They did the same, signaling that they were ready for whatever came for them.

She waited for several breaths before she took another step forward. "I know you are there. Come out now!"

"Sophia," Edric said, hissing her name under his breath.

She didn't respond. Instead, she kept her eyes trained on the moving shadows. These were definitely grimms. Her voice would've startled the minotaurs into attacking. The grimms were more tactful, stealthy, predatory. They hunted their prey. And that's what they were doing now.

She paused and considered that thought. Four grimms, fine. Six? Maybe. But any more than that, and at least one of them was bound to die. Though the nymphs never divulged just how her men died. If she wasn't careful, she'd lose one of them in the Witch Woods tonight. But that wasn't something she was willing to accept. Not now, and possibly not ever. She had to even the odds of the fight just in case there was more than six.

Unwilling to let them die at the hands of ravenous beasts, she rushed into the shadows where she had seen the last movement. A grimm met her. Just as it opened its miasma filled mouth, she ran her sword deep into its throat. A gurgling sound came from the beast as it fell limp, and she pulled her sword from the creature as the others attacked.

Her men rushed forward, and she shouted, "No!"

She would kill them all on her own if she had to. But of course, her men wouldn't listen.

One by one, they fought off the grimms in a nasty, magic-filled fight. Andreas in his wraith form, swooping in and taking on a grimm or two, and Ezekiel with his staff, taking out another. Edric cut a few of them down with his sword.

Sophia landed the final blow in the last grimm and pulled her sword free from the creature's body. When she faced the men, they scowled at her.

"Don't. Ever. Do that again," Edric said. His voice was even, but thick with warning.

"You could've gotten hurt," Andreas said, worry sounded clear in his words.

"Or killed," Ezekiel said.

She took a shuddering breath and said, "I've spent my life training and fighting these creatures. I knew what I was doing. I'm fine. Thankfully, so are you. Now, let's get going."

She swallowed the lump of guilt that threatened to choke her as she turned and headed toward the castle that refused to let her in. This time, she would succeed. She wouldn't accept any other option.

CHAPTER TWELVE

SOPHIA

*S*tanding with her sword at the secret entrance on the back side of the castle, Sophia stared at the faint outline of a door with a slot to the left and center. She mused over what exactly to do with the sword, eventually deciding on holding the tip of the blade to the slot. The blade glowed and responded to her touch in an instant. Touching the tip of the blade to the slot, she gently guided it in.

Nothing.

Her eyebrows knitted together as a pinch formed in her forehead.

"Perhaps," Ezekiel said, "giving it a little twist to the left will work?"

She did that. Still, nothing.

"Try the right," Andreas suggested.

She nodded and did that. Beyond a few clicks, the door still didn't open. "Now what?"

"Push a little of your magic into the sword, then repeat the turns in opposite order," Edric suggested.

But that didn't work either.

Frustrated, Sophia took a deep breath and announced firmly, "Let me in. I bear the sword of the kings!"

A click resounded from the lock, and grinding stone and gears followed. The door opened, revealing a dark tunnel. She gawked at the opening and shifted her gaze to her men who stood looking just as surprised as she was.

"That wasn't in the scroll," Ezekiel said. There was a hint of awe in his voice.

Edric said, "Indeed. You are quite the woman, Sophia." The adoration in his voice made her heart flutter.

"Thank you," she said. "Zeke, a little light?"

He nodded and produced a ball of yellow-white light. Her gaze lingered on the color since normally the witchlight was green. She caught his gaze and he winked. She smiled and shook her head, taking the lead as she and her men stepped into the tunnel.

The door sealed behind them. She stopped and watched as the outside world disappeared. "Well, not that it was an option, but there certainly is no turning back now."

"Something feels off about this tunnel," Edric said.

Ezekiel nodded, "I feel it too."

"It is possible a hidden entrance like this is riddled with traps," Andreas said. "Proceed with caution."

Sophia nodded and returned her attention to the tunnel ahead of them. Despite Ezekiel's light, the darkness was thick, nearly impenetrable. Finding traps would be difficult. But it wasn't long before they came to a fork dividing the tunnel.

"Edric," Sophia said. "You know these tunnels, right?"

"Most of them. This one I can't be sure of," he said. "Zeke, what does the map say?"

Ezekiel handed the ball of light to Sophia and pulled out the map from his satchel. As he studied it, his lips pulled down and he shook his head. "This intersection isn't on the map."

"Great," Sophia said. Of course, this wouldn't be easy. Nothing about this journey was. And with time rapidly running out, she didn't have the convenience of standing by and waiting for the right turn to reveal itself.

Andreas said, "I'll shift and check out each tunnel."

Sophia nodded. "Thank you."

He shifted, and Sophia thought she could never get enough of the awe she felt each time she watched him do so. It was magical, alluring, and she loved that he enjoyed that form so much around her. It was part of who he was, and she loved him even more for that.

Andreas returned and said, "This way is clear."

She nodded. "Thank you. That's where we will go then."

As they headed through the tunnel, Ezekiel was on alert for traps and magical wards, and Sophia kept her eyes opened for any sign of movement while Andreas and Edric covered their backs, making sure no one and nothing followed them.

Close to the end of the tunnel, Edric said, "I recognize where we are."

He took the lead, making his way to a doorway. He held up his hand to signal everyone to stop before cracking open the door. After poking his head around, he stepped into the room. As Sophia entered, she realized it was a room under the stairs, intended for some sort of storage, but appeared to be in disuse.

Edric led them out of the room and around the stairs, each of them looking for signs of trouble. Sophia saw that they were in the castle foyer, and everything was dark, and not a guard was in sight. Not even moonlight filtered in through the towering windows along the front walls. Something about that unnerved Sophia. It seemed too easy to traverse through the castle.

After stepping through another hidden door within the wall of the castle, the door sealed, and a resounding click echoed around them. Gears started turning and it seemed like the walls were narrowing.

They were narrowing!

"Run!" Edric said, and the group dashed forward as fast as they could.

The hall they ran through forced them into single-file as they ran through the ever-closing space with what seemed like too far to go without hope of being crushed. Sophia's heart pounded as she desperately moved to escape the force of the walls, knowing that if she was crushed, the heir to the throne would be lost forever, and Nighthelm would be plunged into darkness.

Ezekiel started to mutter something, and strong wind currents churned between them. Though the winds blasted against the walls, they did little to stop or reverse them from narrowing. He screwed up his face in concentration, but Sophia didn't want to stick around to see if he succeeded in stalling the walls.

"Just keep running!" Sophia said.

Edric was first. Sophia second. Andreas, third. And finally, Ezekiel. Each of them stopped only when they reached a wall. Sophia turned to watch as the hall they were just inside sealed itself. But no alarms sounded, like she expected when a trap was triggered.

Gasping for breath, she shifted her gaze over her men and asked, "Is everyone alright?"

The men nodded as they worked to catch their breath.

"Let's avoid that on the way out," Andreas said. "Shall we?"

"What's the matter, Andreas?" Edric said, "Wraith pancakes not your thing?"

"Ha, ha." Andreas ran his hands over his face and through his hair.

Sophia sighed. "Let's just keep moving."

They walked down the hall, silent as ghosts. Even their breaths didn't make a whisper of sound. As they moved, the hall seemed to go on forever. Sophia worried they had made a wrong turn, but there was none to make after the walls that closed in on them. She took measured breaths to calm her nerves. She took another step, and a click echoed from under her boot.

"Damn," she whispered then quickly ducked out of the way to avoid poison laced spears shooting from the wall on her right.

The acidic tinge mixed with steel was hard to ignore. Though she couldn't tell what sort of poison it was, she could almost taste the metallic, pungent scent that came off the tips of the spears. She dodged three more as she took off in a dead run down the corridor to a T-intersection. Spikes emerged from the walls on the left, so she took the right. Her heart nearly skipped a beat when she tripped over an uneven crack in the ground, but she managed to steady herself and keep herself from getting impaled.

All the while, she listened for three other sets of footsteps behind her. She didn't want her men to get hurt.

More turns appeared in the maze-like passage of the castle, and each turn seemed even more riddled with traps than the last. Finally, she stopped at one intersection and dragged her sword along the wall, which caught on a ridge. If the sword was the key, it would help guide her through the maze. Sinking the blade in, the traps stopped.

Ezekiel's light shone ahead, piercing the thick darkness, catching a metallic design ahead of them.

That was it. That had to be the archives.

"That's it," Edric said, confirming Sophia's thoughts.

Panting for breath, she approached the door and stared at its weird design. It had a lock similar to the one hidden in the castle's outer wall. But instead of being an invisible, magical door, this one was made of wood and steel, with silver filigree that looked disjointed and had no real sense or logic to the design.

Now, she just had to figure out how to open it.

CHAPTER THIRTEEN

SOPHIA

As if traipsing through treacherous, dark tunnels wasn't fun enough. Sophia stood at the door to her next clue to the heir. It was locked. And nothing she did could unlock the damned door. And it didn't seem as though they were as abandoned as she had thought. Someone, or something, was behind that door, shuffling about.

At first, Sophia thought the sound was just her imagination. But she heard it again, and she looked to her men. Each of them held worried expressions. They were all weary from the trek to the archives, and the thought of another fight, if it came down to that, wasn't exactly thrilling.

Sophia tried to use the sword again, this time pushing her magic into it. But it still didn't work.

There had to be a way through the door. She wanted to be careful about how she did it though. She didn't want to trigger another trap. They were so close to getting in, she could practically feel the clue reaching out to her, begging her to reveal it. She had to be careful. This was not a time to rush, despite the time limit proverbially hanging over her head.

She tried one last time to use the sword. More clinking echoed in the hall and she worried she had set off another trap.

"Zeke," she said. And he nodded and turned, facing the end of the hallway, not needing much more direction than just the sound in her voice. He was already working to disarm the trap and find any other magical wards.

Facing the door again, she had no idea what to do. The sword was the key, that's what the nymphs had told her. The sword had to be the way in.

She knelt and studied the shape of the door and the lock. It was similar to the one outside of the castle, but announcing she bore the sword of the kings didn't seem like a good idea. That would probably draw too much attention to them. They needed to be stealthy and quick. That meant drawing attention could spell trouble for them, and they already had their fair share of traps on their unexpectedly deadly trek here to begin with.

The filigree had to have something to do with the

lock. She tried to force them to move with her hand, setting off more traps. She tried moving them in a pattern. That didn't work.

Sighing, frustrated, she stood back and stared at the door, willing the solution to come to her. The only thing she hadn't done was hang the sword on the door. Figuring it was an option worth trying, she would rather attempt it than straight out dismiss it. She placed the sword on the door, hilt up, and blade tip pointed downward.

The filigree moved, connecting in a weird, jagged circle, that when complete, dispersed an aura from the center of the sword. The lock clicked and the door slid open a crack.

She stared at the door almost too nervous to push it open. But this was what she fought and nearly died for. Now was not the time for second-guessing.

"Good work," Edric said.

She nodded. "Let's split up. Andreas and Edric, you search the back end. Zeke and I will search the front. We'll check back if we find anything."

With a nod from the men, Sophia pushed the door all the way open and peeked inside. Whoever or what-ever was in the room before must have left. Or perhaps it was a draft. The area held an almost unnat-ural chill that seemed to move through the room.

Shaking off that feeling, she moved to the first shelf in the archive, which turned out to be little more than a large storage room filled with books, scrolls, and a whole lot of dust and melted wax. It wasn't the most glamorous of places, but she was certain they would find the next clue here. It *had* to be here, otherwise they'd run out of time and lose the heir forever.

CHAPTER FOURTEEN

ANDREAS

*A*ndreas went to one of the nearest shelves toward the back of the archive and thumbed through some of the old scrolls and tomes, looking for anything that could be of use. A strange sensation of being watched overcame him. He turned, hand on his sword, only to find dust, shadow, and shelves full of tomes.

Being a creature of darkness and shadow, he could sense something dark nearby. They didn't have much time there, and what little they did was rapidly running out. They needed to quickly find the information they needed and get out of there.

Shaking off his initial alarm and removing his hand from the hilt of his sword, he returned to his search. Albeit, a little faster now. He knew that if the duchess found out they were there, they would never get another chance in the archives. Not to mention there would be some pretty deep shit to pay for.

His mind returned to the mountain and the vexsnare that had hunted them. Forcing back a shudder, he forced himself to focus. He didn't think the mountain would be an option the next time they were caught. And he hated to think of the only other fate they would face.

Edric rounded the corner and said, "I can't find anything. I hope you're having more luck than I."

Andreas shook his head. They exchanged a worried glance. He knew this was a possible dead end. "Hopefully Zeke and Sophia are having better luck."

"I certainly hope so," Edric said. "I would hate to go through all this trouble only to come up empty-handed."

Andreas said, "For Sophia's sake, let's hope there's at least something here."

"Agreed," Edric said. "Perhaps we should regroup or trade off. Another look through the shelves with different eyes may help turn up something that was initially overlooked."

Andreas agreed and went to the back shelves Edric had already gone through. At this point, anything was worth a shot. After all, getting to the archives was difficult enough. And it would be nice to have something come easy for once.

Not finding anything, he decided to go check on

Sophia. He found her searching through the endless scrolls and parchments of old.

"Finding anything?" he asked.

She sighed and shook her head. "You?"

"Nothing yet. I'll keep looking though." He smiled and hoped that it reassured her, just a little. He could tell she was tense and worried with not having found anything of use yet.

She returned his smile and said, "Good luck."

He nodded and went to find Ezekiel. Perhaps he had better luck, if he didn't get carried away with the thrill of the tomes he had yet to read.

EZEKIEL

*E*zekiel was in heaven.

A desperate urge to finger through the tomes, parchments, and scrolls kept safe from years of study with the most powerful sorcerers of his past overcame him. It nearly overwhelmed him with need.

Instead of giving in though, he kept his focus on Sophia's quest. Anything that he could find to help her in restoring the last remaining heir, he would do. Perhaps, he would find something that would be of use for him in the future, but he wouldn't be able to live with the guilt of dividing his focus.

But despite the everlasting researcher in him begging him to pick a scroll, any scroll, he scanned the spines of the tomes for anything that would point toward the heirs. His search was looking bleak, but he pressed on.

Andreas rounded the corner. Ezekiel met his gaze. Andreas nodded. "Find anything?"

"Other than a gripping need to stay here for the rest of my life studying the scrolls? Nope. I'm not willing to give up yet, though." He said through a heavy breath. "What about you? Find anything yet?"

Andreas shook his head. "This can't be a worthless clue."

"I agree. Something has to be here." Ezekiel pulled out a tome missing its title, likely worn off from years of use and then disuse. He flipped through the pages, but it turned out to be a historical retelling of the gods and their sleeping habits. He replaced it.

"Maybe Sophia has had better luck," Andreas said.

"I sure hope so," Ezekiel muttered.

Hope dwindled more and more, with each moment spent finding nothing leading to the heir. He didn't know what he would do to comfort Sophia if that ended up being the case. He had to keep what little hope he had left alive. Otherwise, the point of this whole thing was moot. And he just couldn't believe that.

CHAPTER FIFTEEN

SOPHIA

*S*ophia was frustrated.

So far, everything was turning up a whole lot of nothing. She figured she misunderstood what the nymphs were hinting at, or they were just less forward with the information she needed than she originally thought. Either way, she refused to give up on the search until every little nook and cranny had been explored.

In a last-stitch effort, she pulled on the sword, held the blade against her forehead, and sighed. She put as much need and desperation into her words as possible. She couldn't believe that this trip was a dead end. "Please, you have gotten me this far, guiding me to this point. Don't fail me now."

A pull in the center of her gut urged her forward

toward the wall. Trusting in the sensation, she continued to walk, following the pull to an alcove.

She spotted something hidden behind tall shelves and layers of thick dust in the farthest corner of the archives. A rumpled up, dingy white cloth, stained from years of neglect, sat covering something meant to be kept secret. Pulling on the cloth, she discovered a collection of paintings.

She pulled one into the light and studied the image before her. Her heartbeats pounded in her ears. Her breath came in short bursts, and her body tingled.

The king stood proudly next to his queen. Two little girls stood before them. The king rested a loving hand on the shoulder of his daughter while she held her head high, heir to the throne with a brilliant, jeweled tiara resting on her head. The other little girl, younger than the first, stood in front of the queen. Though she didn't have a tiara, she also stood proud, smiling wide, looking happy and loved.

Sophia's lips pulled into their own smile, a soft, almost sad, one. She wished she had known her own family. Known what it was like to have that love and pride.

Refocus.

This was the closest she had ever been to a solid clue on what the heirs looked like. She stared at the two girls, wondering which one still lived and which one had unfortunately perished. As she studied the tallest one, Sophia believed her to be the strongest and most apt to have survived the mountain and whatever killed the other. She held the air of nobility, standing proudly before her father, the king.

She seemed familiar though. But Sophia couldn't place why.

The other girl…

Wait.

The older one…

She looked just like…

The long, golden-brown hair that curled around the familiar shape of the girl's face. The arch of her eyebrows and fullness of her lips…

Sophia sucked in a breath that got caught in her throat. The girl in the painting looked just like the one in the coffin. Just younger. Much younger.

No. It couldn't be. Could it?

Ezekiel stepped up behind her. She leaned into him, but she couldn't bring herself to take her eyes off the girl in the painting.

"Wow," he said. "She looks just like the girl we found."

Sophia's voice was as soft as a whisper. "I think that's because it *is* her."

She finally pulled her eyes from the painting to turn and face Ezekiel. He stared at the painting. His eyes grew wide as the realization dawned on him.

"I didn't see that one coming." He ran a hand

through his hair. "I always thought the heir was a man. After all, Nighthelm held an extensive line of kings with boys as heirs. Not girls."

Sophia nodded. "Maybe because everyone assumed the heirs were male, in order to protect the princesses, the king and queen let people think so."

Ezekiel scratched his chin. "Very possible. Who knows how long a plot to take out the royal family had been in the works and if the king and queen even knew about it."

She returned to face the painting and ran the tip of her fingers across the other girl's image. A mix of anger and sadness consumed her. Her magic buzzed through her, but she kept it down. With everything in her, she knew the eldest princess was the last remaining heir, laid in a crystal coffin within the caves of Ripthorn.

Andreas and Edric joined her and Ezekiel. Edric was holding a book.

Sophia asked, "What did you find?"

"A book of records," he said. "We assume it is a birth record of the most recent bloodline in Nighthelm royalty."

"That may be useful. We can learn the name of the heir at least," Ezekiel said and took up the book and began flipping through the pages.

"What did you find?" Andreas asked.

Sophia pointed to the painting behind her. "We found the heir."

CHAPTER SIXTEEN

SOPHIA

Sophia had found the heir.

She just didn't quite know how she, herself, fit into everything just yet.

The oracles told her to find the missing pieces of her soul. She would be healed. They also said she wasn't meant to be a slave or a warrior, and that she was an orphan lost in the mountain. The last thing they told her was to restore the throne.

Ripthorn seemed to have a lot to do with her and her past. The mountain held the last living heir as well.

The nymphs told her the magic keeping the heir alive was dwindling away. They had a little over a week to find her, the key to waking her, and then they would finally restore her to the throne. Her destiny would finally be fulfilled. She hoped she would live in peace with her men after that. As long as she had them by her side, she would be happy. Even on days when it seemed the odds were against them.

She frowned.

It did no one any good standing around. She reached for the book Edric still held. He handed it over and she flipped through the pages, just for added measure. A good chunk of the last half remained empty. The last name scrawled onto the page was Madison Averell. She stared at the girl in the painting, repeating her name over and over in her mind. Somehow, she knew this girl, but she couldn't place how. And it confirmed that she was the girl in the painting.

There was no entry for the other girl in the painting. Knowing something horrible happened to the younger girl pained Sophia. She couldn't imagine the horrors that the poor child faced and the ghastly death she had to endure.

Shaking her head, she returned her attention to the older girl. Sophia tapped the name on the page. "Her name is Madison Averell. There is no name listed for the other girl in the painting. Whoever she is, still remains a mystery."

"You're certain this is the heir?" Edric said.

Sophia nodded. "With everything I have."

Edric said, "I got to say that this is surprising. All this time I thought we were searching for a male heir."

"I said the same!" Ezekiel said.

"Focus," Sophia said. "We need to get Madison healed and out of that coffin. Time is running out."

"First," Edric said, "We need to get back. We can plan our next step back in the village."

"Leaving so soon?" a woman's voice spoke from behind them.

Sophia turned and settled her eyes on the duchess, standing regally in the doorway of the archives. Her dress was dark—navy blue or black, Sophia couldn't tell which—with silver brocade and lace. Her head was adorned with a crown that angered Sophia more each time she saw it on the woman's head.

"You just arrived, after all. And it would be rude not to at least say hi." She examined her nails then set her cold gaze on Sophia and her men.

"You're in danger," Sophia said.

The duchess laughed. "Quite. I have the city's most wanted criminals in my sight."

"No." Sophia sighed. "The Nameless Master is after you."

"Dear girl, let me explain something to you. I'm as safe as safe can be. Even from the Nameless Master. And once you are dealt with, I'll ensure that this little secret you have stumbled upon dies with you."

Sophia's gut tightened into a knot. Her men stiffened and Edric's hand went to the hilt of his sword. She quickly put the pieces together and realized that she somehow had something to do with the heirs disappearing.

"What have you done?"

The duchess quirked an eye brow as she stood taller with her chin held in the air. "What I had to do."

"You... you killed them?" Though Sophia didn't mean for it to come out as a question, it had. And her voice sounded foreign to her own ears. As though she didn't want to believe the truth despite everything in her body knowing it beyond any doubt.

"It's a shame you didn't remain ignorant to the heir. I had such hopes for you." She sighed. "No matter. It's not like the royal family is going to suddenly appear alive and well. You'll be joining them now. Send them my regards."

Sophia realized the duchess must not have overheard much of their conversation. Especially the part about reviving Madison and restoring her to the throne. For now, the heir was safe. And though she didn't know what the Nameless Master wanted with the duchess, Sophia was now sure that they were working together. The power-hungry duchess probably made some type of deal with the Nameless Master that would assure her the throne and the royal family out of the way.

With a flick of her hand, the duchess released traps within the room, which resounded with clicks and the sound of grinding gears and chains. She darted into the dark corridor and said, "Now the throne will finally be mine!"

"Damn," Andreas said.

Green, toxic mist floated through cracks in the walls, covering the floor. Poisoned gas. Sophia shook her head as gears and chains continued to move behind the stone. Knowing her luck, it would be more moving walls, sealing them in the room.

They had to escape and fast. But with a quick look around, the only way in and out of the room was through that one door.

That would have to do.

"Hold your breath," she said.

Jumping into action, Sophia darted into the hallway, pulling on the sword, and her men following close behind her.

Her eyes darted along the hall. She knew the duchess had just gone this way, but the castle would know to stop them, and the traps would make the trek even more difficult. Spikes jutted up from the floor right in front of Sophia. She stopped mid-run, narrowly missing being skewered alive.

Once the spikes withdrew into the floor again, Sophia hunted for the trigger. If there was one set of spikes, she had no doubt others were along the floors.

"Keep close to the walls to avoid the spikes," she said as she dragged her sword along the wall. It worked the first time, and she hoped this time was no different. The sword glowed bright white and illuminated the walls on either side of her.

She angled the sword to aim the beam in front of her and saw a switch used to automate the traps. But when she approached it, spikes shot down from the ceiling and nearly made her day go from bad to worse. Even still, the switch looked like it had been crushed and the center portion of it was missing.

"The switch is broken," she said.

Ezekiel approached, avoiding the spikes as well. He studied the switch and shook his head. "I can't do anything with that."

"Use the sword," Edric suggested.

"I'll go forward and see what other switches are in sight, and maybe we can take them out as we go," Andreas said and shifted into wraith form.

Sophia asked, "Use the sword how?"

"Cut the switch from the wall," Edric said. "It will relieve the pressure triggering the traps."

Sophia hadn't thought of that, and it was a great idea. Angling herself awkwardly against the wall, she lifted the sword into the air and brought it down against the switch. The stone and wooden contraption shattered. A loud twang echoed, as though a spring was released, and the traps stopped, receding into their deadly holes.

She released a sigh of relief and took stock of the next set of traps that could pop up at the most inopportune moment. Meanwhile, she kept an eye out for Andreas, hoping he would return soon. After all, they couldn't stay in the belly of the castle, hidden in its secretive walls forever. They needed to get out, get to the camp, and set a plan to rescue Madison.

After several long minutes and still no sign of Andreas, Sophia turned to Edric and Ezekiel. "Let's go find him."

Slowly, and very carefully, they headed farther down the hallway, keeping an eye out for not only Andreas in his wraith form, but also any traps.

As they moved, something didn't seem right. Things looked... different. Sophia couldn't place how or why, but it did. And as she came up to a dead end, she knew for sure that the castle was rearranging itself to keep them from getting out.

Edric examined the wall while Sophia asked, "Is there a way out back behind us?"

Ezekiel shook his head. "It's possible this is why Andreas hasn't come back yet."

"He knows to go back to the wraith camp. In case we are separated further, that's where we will meet up. Hopefully, we will find him on the way without anymore issues, and we can all go together," Sophia said.

Edric grunted as he tried to push on the wall. "Damn it. It's like the wall was built here, but I know it wasn't."

"It's the castle. It's trying to keep us from escaping," Sophia said. "It had done something similar one night when I was trying to get in to find information on the heirs, just after meeting the three of you."

"I knew the castle had such defenses on the outside, but not within," Edric said.

"Well, now we all know," Ezekiel said. "Let's back track."

"Good idea," Sophia said. "There has to be a way out somewhere."

They turned and followed Ezekiel back toward the way they just came from. He stopped suddenly. Sophia bumped into him and had to quickly grab hold of the back of his shirt to keep him from toppling over into a deep, black pit.

They were blocked from getting any farther, and it seemed like they were stuck. Sophia leaned against a wall and sighed. Edric did the same on the opposite wall. The wall shifted inward. He lost his footing, falling into the room on the other side. Sophia went to go pull him back as the wall started to close. But it was too late. The door sealed.

The last thing she saw was Edric staring up at them with an expression of horror mixed with shock.

She hit the wall with the sides of her fists. Was this how she'd lose her men? In the bowels of the castle, each of them being swallowed or caught in deadly traps?

Ezekiel laid a gentle hand on her shoulder. "We should continue. He knows the castle well enough, and he also knows to meet us at the camp."

Sophia took several deep breaths to ease the anger inside her. She should have saved him. She should have grabbed him and pulled him out of the way.

"Think of it this way," Ezekiel said, "now we know the walls are trapped like that. We can stay away from them and hopefully avoid being separated even more."

His voice was calm and soothing, but it didn't help Sophia's nerves. She would continue to worry until she saw them again. For now, she focused on keeping Ezekiel in her sight.

Sword at the ready, she walked back the opposite direction, away from the pit, stopping at yet another one.

Frustration burned through her nerves and her magic coursed through her veins. This looked like a hopeless situation, and she was done being toyed with by a castle and the duchess's stupid traps.

The sword pulsed with light and magic and she paused to look at it, an idea forming in her mind.

The sword was the key to getting into the castle, through the door to the archives, and even to stopping some of the traps on the way there. Looking around, she searched for a slot, bump, hole—*anything*—that would stop the traps and let them out of the castle. Finding Edric and Andreas on the way would be a bonus she hoped for. But first, she needed to find the way to stop the traps. And quickly.

With the flat end of the blade, she tapped the floor where the trap was, testing the flooring surrounding it and hoping that the vibration would trigger it to close.

Nothing happened.

She pushed her magic into the sword. It glowed brighter, pulsating with energy. Across from her on a wall opposite of the pit, a keyhole shone bright purple.

That must've been it.

Now, how to get across.

She looked behind her and judged the space between pits. She knew the more they moved, the more likely it was for another pit to reveal itself. But if she could get enough of a running start, she could jump over the first pit and get the sword into the keyhole hopefully before any more traps were triggered.

"What are you thinking?" Ezekiel asked.

She met his gaze and she said, "Jumping."

His eyebrows pinched together, and he looked across the way. He seemed to have come to the same conclusion. He nodded. "I'll stand here. There should be enough room for you to jump several paces back. That should, in theory, prevent the trap from being triggered."

Sophia nodded then took several paces back. Holding her sword with the tip pointed up at an angle, she pushed off with her feet. As she arrived at the edge of the first pit, she thrusted herself into the air. Her feet hit the solid ground, and another trap was triggered. Slats from the wall on either side of the keyhole opened up.

Darts shot from the sections.

She dodged each, ducking and rolling out of the way and twisting to avoid getting impaled by one. A slice of heat pierced her upper arm and she winced but kept moving. Another dart cut into her thigh.

Biting against the pain, she reached the keyhole and slid the sword in. She twisted both ways and a resounding click echoed before the darts ceased, sealing behind the slats once more. Panting, she turned and found Ezekiel walking toward her. Once he reached her, he cupped her face and planted a kiss on her lips.

"Smart girl," he said and smiled. "Now, let's get out of here."

She nodded and they ran for it, working through the many twists and turns. Each trap they came across, Sophia used the sword to disarm them.

Once they reached a bend, Ezekiel recognized where they were. "This way, there is a gate that opens into Witch Woods."

"Do you think Andreas and Edric made it out?" Sophia asked as she followed him down the hall to the gate.

"Yes," he said. But she was sure it was said to reassure her more than anything.

Up ahead, she saw shadows moving. Ezekiel stopped running and held up his hand. She stopped and they narrowed their eyes on the movements.

After exchanging a glance and a nod, Ezekiel and Sophia made their way slower, careful not to make a sound, toward the shadows. Whoever it was had been waiting for them, and Sophia refused to go down without a fight.

She aimed her sword, ready to make the kill as she drew closer.

"Sophia?" Andreas asked.

That halted her steps and her heart skipped a beat. She released the breath she had been holding and rushed into his arms. The other shadow was Edric. They each took turns hugging or shaking hands.

"I thought the worst had happened to you both," Edric said.

"I too worried," Sophia said. "Let's get out of here before we have to go through that again."

The men agreed. They all rushed into the woods, heading for the wraith village.

CHAPTER SEVENTEEN

SOPHIA

*W*ithout wasting time, Sophia and her men rushed into the village. Andreas went to gather as many wraiths as he could to help with carrying Madison out of the mountain, while Ezekiel gathered his notes and supplies to help curb the effects of the mountain's magic. They still had the amulets, and Sophia hoped they would work long enough for them to get in and get out. Edric gathered what rations they would need, and Sophia scouted ahead for a way through to the mountain without getting caught by grimms using the masking potion Ezekiel had made for their trip to the nymphs.

Once she found the path, she returned, and they set off.

Finding the cave wasn't as difficult as she thought it would be.

Using magic, Ezekiel and Sophia widened the exit by shattering the larger boulders that were in the way. The pieces fell to the ground, sizzling like hot coals. The wraiths moved in with their shadowy forms, floating effortlessly like a large cloud. They shifted and hovered in the air. Sophia listened for any creatures or attackers outside of the cave as the wraiths carefully floated the crystal coffin on their backs.

Once they were out in the daylight, Ezekiel examined the coffin for any cracks. Sophia watched as he traced his fingers along the base. She held her breath, hoping there was a secret to waking her within the symbols etched into the crystal. She worried they would inevitably be too late, but she also maintained hope that they would make it back in once piece, unscathed, and would have the heir awake. She wondered what she would be like and if the girl knew what had happened to her. It was almost painful to see the heir lying in such a death-like state. Knowing the duchess was responsible for all this mess, she would make her pay for that, and more.

"These runes were placed here to prevent tampering and would promise a very painful experience to anyone trying to open it without the key."

Great.

Of course, there would be something else to stand in their way.

Sophia nodded. "Stay on top of it. See what you can figure out by the time we get back to the village."

"I'll write down all my findings. They are in code as well. Similar to the ones in the scroll. It is possible they coordinate, and the key is within the scroll's message."

Moving carefully through the mountain, they carried the heir to Nighthelm, hoping beyond all hope that they would get back without a fight.

Just when Sophia could see the edge of the Witch Woods, a giant shadow shifted through the darkness. Her body alert, she pulled on her sword right as the giant lizard-like creature emerged from the tree line.

It was beyond monstrous. Instead of skin, it seemed to be created from a series of roots and branches, with tops of trees lining its back from the base of its head to its tail. Its eyes were like yellow moons and were focused right on them.

The creature swished its branchy tail toward them, narrowly missing their group by inches.

The wraiths carrying Madison floated back several yards and carefully sat her down before joining the fight.

They coordinated with each other, flanking the creature and dispatching it quickly with fire and a whole lot of stabbing between the knots and weaved wood. It fell with a deafening roar, and Sophia's muscles ached from the exertion of the fight. But she refused to let any creature or force stand in her way, not when she was so close to fulfilling her destiny. She would keep fighting, for the heir and for those she loved.

Sophia checked on her men to make sure they weren't harmed and that Ezekiel and Edric were holding up well against the poisonous mountain magic.

Their amulets were charged with a slight glow, but she could tell that they were wearing thin. She knew they had to get out of the mountain, but she also realized they needed rest.

"Let's make camp for the night. Resume in the morning," she said. The amulets would at least hold out until then.

The wraiths almost looked relieved, and Edric immediately started laying out his bedroll. After that battle with the lizard creature, they all could use the night to recover. Andreas and another wraith volunteered for first watch, which gave the others time to set up a fire and make food. Ezekiel took the opportunity to research the runes and his notes. Sophia sat next to him.

"Anything good yet?" she asked.

He pointed to one rune and said, "This one sticks out. It's not as obvious as the scroll was, but I do believe the same code applies. It's just a matter of figuring out the key to the code and solving from there."

She nodded. "Anything I can do to help?"

He shook his head then kissed her on the cheek. "Lay down and rest, woman."

She smiled, but resting was the furthest thing from her mind. Still, she lay next to him and stared at the starry sky through a hole within the rock of Riphthorn.

"Are you feeling all right?" she asked him.

He nodded and "mm-hmmed."

She knew he was starting to feel the effects of the mountain magic despite the amulet. He was just trying to keep her from worrying. She could appreciate that about him. Returning her gaze to the ceiling, she became restless and decided to stand and do some stretches. Walk around the perimeter of the camp to help keep watch.

"Sophia, I found something," Ezekiel called to her, and she rushed over to find out the news. "I think I found something. There is mention of an herb called Animo's Passion. It holds some powerful healing and restoration attributes. It's rare, and only found within certain elements. I believe there to be some deep within Witch Woods around a fairy den as they tend to use the berries as aphrodisiacs."

Fairy den. That meant there would be a fight. Despite the pesky creatures that they were, it was so worth the risk. This was the only shot they had so far of waking Madison, and she wasn't going to wait around for another option. "Fairies are particularly possessive of things they value. It would likely mean a fight, but we can handle it."

"When should we leave?"

"You up for it tonight?" she asked.

He nodded. "I think we could do it."

"Great. I'll go let Edric and Andreas know. They can handle guarding the queen."

She turned and headed for Edric and Andreas.

CHAPTER EIGHTEEN

ANDREAS

$\mathcal{H}$e watched as Sophia approached him. Something about the determined look in her eyes gave him the impression she wasn't approaching with the intent of spending time with him. There was something more behind it.

She stopped in front of him and smiled. "Hi."

"Hello," he said, smiling back.

"Zeke found information about an herb that can revive Madison. I'm going to leave with him to go get it. I'm leaving you and Edric in charge of getting the queen back to the village and watching over her."

"You're leaving now?" he asked, somewhat shocked, though he knew not to be. Nothing was predictable about this woman. Even now. Probably ever.

She narrowed her eyes and her eyebrows met at

the bridge of her nose. Her rather cute nose. "Yes. It's our best shot at waking her without killing her completely."

"Let me get two of my wraith brothers to accompany you in case there's trouble," Andreas said and went to leave her.

She stopped him by grabbing his arm. "No. The less company we bring with us, the more we can stay hidden."

"Grimms, Sophia. Remember?" He couldn't hide the worry in his voice.

"I'll be fine. Zeke is with me, and Haris as well." She showed her forearm. "Besides, I've handled worse than a few run-ins with grimms and a den of fairies."

"Please consider taking two at least," he said, urging her to compromise.

She shook her head and rested an arm on his shoulder. "It will be better and quicker with just the two of us. We'll be back as soon as possible."

She lifted up on her toes and pressed her lips to his. He returned the kiss and pulled her closer to him. When he broke away, he rested his head against hers. "Please, be careful."

"Always," she said then walked away.

He watched her as she and Ezekiel stepped into the woods under the cover of night. Once they left his sight, he turned to the heir and wondered why the duchess would want power so badly that she would go through all the trouble of killing the entire royal family. His thoughts led into wondering who went out of their way to save Madison in such an intricate and careful way. There was a lot of thought put into something that seemed to have happened so rapidly.

He hummed to himself.

There was definitely more to this whole scenario than met the eye, and he was sure the heir would provide answers once she was up and well.

He just hoped that Sophia and Ezekiel didn't see any trouble while they were gone. Or the group left behind for that matter.

Edric stretched as he walked toward Andreas. He could tell the magic was starting to affect him, and he frowned noticing Edric's skin had paled a few shades in the short time they were here.

"Get good rest?" Andreas asked as Edric stood next to him.

He shrugged. "About as good as I'm going to get for the time being."

"I'm right there with you, brother," he said, slapping a hand on his shoulder and giving it a squeeze.

"Somehow, I highly doubt that. Your people are from here, after all." His voice was level, but there was a hint of pain and Andreas frowned, removing his hand. Sophia would never forgive him if something happened to Edric while she was gone.

Silence settled between them as they both studied the crystal coffin that held the last heir of Nighthelm.

"Why do you think she did it?" Andreas asked.

"Who? The duchess?" He shrugged. "I have no clue. Maybe she didn't. Maybe it was someone else and she was just a pawn in the whole scheme. She doesn't seem like the type to kill."

"Possible." Andreas shifted his weight between his feet, circulating his blood from standing so long. "Even Winston surprised us with his baffling exploit to take Sophia from us."

"True. Proves the point that you never really know a person until you know what drives them and pushes them to do the things they do."

Somehow, that reminded him of Sophia and her determination to get the heir on the throne. He knew the desire to fulfill her destiny motivated her, though it seemed lately something else had been bothering her.

"Agreed. Have you noticed a change in Sophia lately?"

"What do you mean?" Edric asked.

"She's more vigilant, focused… maybe more intense than usual."

He shrugged. "She's closer than ever to restoring the heir. She's likely pushing herself to get that done. She has a time limit as well. That tends to place a lot of weight on her shoulders." He met Andreas's gaze. "Relax, brother. She'll be fine."

"Fair enough," Andreas said and watched the movements of shadows and wraiths.

"We should change the watch and leave out early. Hopefully we can beat Sophia and Zeke back to the village and have Madison ready to be awakened."

"Good point," Andreas said and watched as Edric set off to find two wraiths to take over the watch.

∽

EDRIC

He took guard over the woods. He felt trouble inching over the horizon. It was coming. That was beyond a doubt. Somehow, he also knew getting Madison back on the throne was going to take a lot more effort. The duchess had grown too comfortable in her position, and with her admitting she was responsible for killing off the royal family in the first place, and trying to kill him, his brothers, and Sophia just to maintain that throne, she wouldn't let go without force.

Madison would need to be prepared to do something big to prove herself the heir. Even then, he wondered what would stop the mastermind behind the murders of the royal family from completing the task once she was awake and reclaimed the throne. He still couldn't believe the duchess had anything to do with it, and he pondered whether or not she had a co-conspirator.

As his eyes scanned for each and every shift of shadow within the dense trees of Witch Woods, he thought back to his younger years, when he was a boy at the academy and the stories he'd hear of how the royal family had special skills. Though he never learned what those skills were, he hoped that would be enough to prove Madison's right to the throne. And once she did, he could reclaim his position within the guard and set up an elite force that would protect the queen around the clock. Before he got too far ahead of himself, they needed to first wake her up.

Sophia and Ezekiel needed to hurry. Whatever was out there in those woods, Edric sensed it was out for blood. And the blood of the heir, Madison.

CHAPTER NINETEEN

SOPHIA

*S*ophia and Ezekiel were making good time. They had run quite a way once they crossed into the barrier of the woods and had only stopped to catch their breath and allow Ezekiel to look around for signs of the plant and fairies.

"*Vocavi*," she whispered.

Haris's form filtered from her arm, moving in front of her in his brilliant green mist, solidifying with a grateful sigh. He nudged her and trilled.

She chuckled and patted his flank. "You're welcome, my friend."

Ezekiel stared at the moss on the trees and searched around him. "Not quite there yet. But I believe we are getting close."

"Do you really think the herb will be enough?" Sophia asked as she followed Ezekiel deeper into the woods. She kept her voice low as to not draw attention from unwanted creatures. They had a time limit, and a fight with a minotaur, grimm, or other dangerous creatures of the woods would only slow them down.

Time was of the essence.

"It should. It has to." Ezekiel fingered some ferns growing alongside a toppled over branch. He rubbed some of the moist soil between his first two fingers and thumb then sniffed. "Too acidic."

"Not to mention there aren't any fairy nests nearby." Sophia poked Ezekiel in the side and pointed ahead of them where there were glowing plants.

He smiled. "You never cease to amaze me."

She smiled and mock bowed. "Anything for you."

He chuckled and headed for the glowing plant life. Sophia knew that was a fairly large den of fairies. It was worth a shot to check, seeing as it was the first one they had seen. It was a decently secluded series of nests as well. Sophia had no idea what conditions needed to be present for the plant to grow, but this was pretty deep in the woods and the dim glow of the plants caught her attention. Fairies loved pretty, glowing things.

Ezekiel asked, "What do you think we're going to do once we restore Madison to the throne? You know, after your destiny is fulfilled."

"Sleep and enjoy the peace for however long we're allowed to have it," she said.

She had spent much of her life fighting and training to be a warrior. But even warriors needed rest, and her victory with Madison would help her achieve that. Sometimes she would catch herself daydreaming about what she'd do with her men, on a normal day, when they weren't called upon to go to battle. But now wasn't the time to dwell on possibilities. It was a time for action. And Sophia would find the herb to wake Madison and restore her to the throne. Nighthelm had gone for too long without its rightful heir.

"I want to buy a house for all of us. Or restore the estate. Have a library where I can return to the archives and research." Ezekiel's voice was full of desire and awe. It took everything within Sophia not to laugh loudly at the way he always seemed obsessed with learning more. It was endearing to her as well. He didn't speak too often about his wants and dreams. It gave her a little more insight to him, which she craved.

"You love learning that much?" she asked.

He nodded and smiled. "It's what I do. Why I'm so good at magic."

"That makes sense."

Sophia grabbed his hand and they walked casually toward the glowing plants. They spent the rest of the time in silence. Every few steps, Ezekiel stopped to touch moss or rub dirt between his fingers. Once, he pulled a petal off a flower and tasted it. He rapidly spat it out and muttered something about being bitter. Sophia tried not to laugh, but what sound she did make, she managed to muffle behind her hands.

He could always make her laugh. She felt carefree with him and enjoyed that he could take a serious situation and bring some humor into it. She really loved that about him, and each day, she found herself falling in love with him even deeper.

Haris sniffed the flower Ezekiel had just spat out and snorted, shaking his head, almost bumping into trees.

"Now he tells me," Ezekiel said.

Sophia forced herself to muffle another chuckle as she set her eyes forward and saw the tiny tells of fairy homes littered throughout the trunk of nearby trees.

It was late, so they were likely sleeping. Not many of the creatures were nocturnal, and the ones who were tended to be more ferocious, highly disliking of trespassers into their territory. Their bites seemed worse than the others, but it was something Sophia was prepared for.

But as they snuck into the den, quiet as ghosts, she was surprised to find a whole lot of nothing but the soft whispers of a breeze gently brushing against the leaves of the tress and a trickling stream nearby.

"We're close," Ezekiel whispered.

Sophia nodded and pulled on the hilts of her dagger and sword, prepared for an onslaught of tiny, angry creatures for disturbing their loot.

"Over here," Ezekiel whispered again, and she followed him to a small bush about three feet high with bright white flowers that looked like little, spiny snowballs with purple berries. The whole herb glowed and reminded Sophia of a collection of stars when she was able to view them from one of the rooftops in Nighthelm during one of her many treks into the city at night. That was before Grindel died, and she had met her men that she had come to adore.

The silence was almost deafening. And Sophia started to think things were going easy.

Ezekiel took out a small blade and cut a flower from the bush. It made a loud snipping sound that echoed, causing Sophia to suck in a breath and look around.

A collection of buzzing burst through the nests as she, Ezekiel, and Haris were swarmed by the tiny creatures.

Using the flat side of her blade, she batted at the fairies attacking her and used the dagger to take out a few others. Ezekiel used a flickering flame in the palm of his hand and kept the creatures at bay so he could collect the herbs.

Haris stomped around and spun, trying to knock

as many of them off as possible. He groaned each time one of them bit into him, and Sophia tried her best to keep them from biting her as she knocked them off him.

They seemed to have come from all directions, and though she didn't want to completely demolish an entire den of fairies, she would do so to make sure Ezekiel grabbed enough of the herb to wake Madison up.

"Got it! Let's go," Ezekiel announced, and like the wind, they dashed through the woods, making their way back to the village.

CHAPTER TWENTY

SOPHIA

*A*s they stepped into the village, Sophia and Ezekiel were laughing about the fairy attack. She teased him about his rapid movements and wide eyes, almost like a scared child lashing out at the nightmares that loomed under his bed. The adrenaline pumping through her veins had finally waned, and after the initial shock of being besieged by biting fairies, being in such a situation—a trained warrior and a skilled sorcerer—just brought out a bit of humor in them. Ezekiel had made some jokes of his own, pointing out the way in which she batted away several of the fairies.

But as they rejoined Andreas and Edric, Sophia became serious. "How is the heir?"

"We put her in a hut over there," Andreas said,

pointing to the very hut that held the chest protected by the cute little gnome.

She instantly turned on her heels and headed in that direction. As she set her eyes on the heir, she whispered, "Thank the gods." The tension in her shoulder eased, and she moved to stand to the side. She looked at the girl, Madison, and wondered if she dreamed in this state, or if she was somehow aware of her surroundings.

"Did you get the herbs?" Edric asked Ezekiel.

"I did. I just need a moment to prepare the potion," he said.

Sophia smiled but was also weary. It was a long fight just to get to this moment, and she was sure there would be plenty more battles to come to get the heir healed, awake, and on the throne.

"We should set up watch around the heir as well as the village," Sophia said.

"Already done," Edric said, walking up behind her and resting his hands on her shoulders.

She closed her eyes and leaned into him.

Now they waited for Ezekiel to work his magic. Both figuratively and literally.

SOPHIA

*S*ophia's nerves were on edge.

Pacing the length of the village didn't help ease her or bring her comfort. Too much was riding on Ezekiel finding a clue to opening the coffin without killing the last heir to the throne.

Her thoughts didn't help matters either. She was consumed with wondering how she got in the crystal coffin in the first place. Who put her in there? How in the world were they going to get her back on the throne? What if they messed up and killed her?

Too much.

She eventually grew tired of pacing and went to check on him, finding him hunched over his book of notes, pencil in hand, scribbling furiously. She cleared her throat to announce her arrival without startling him.

He looked up from his notes and smiled.

"How is everything coming along?" she asked.

"I'm getting close," he said. "I can feel it."

"Can I sit next to you?" she asked.

He returned his attention to her and his eyebrows knitted together. "Do you really need to ask?"

She shrugged and he patted the spot next to him.

Taking the seat, she looked at the notes in his book and couldn't make heads or tails of anything on there. It was just a mesh of symbols that looked more like an interesting art project than a language.

"How can you understand any of that?" she asked.

"Simple," he said. "Many, many years of practice. I started learning the ancient text my first year at the academy. It fascinated me so much I couldn't leave the subject alone. I still don't know everything. Some runes change meaning, depending on where they appear. Others could be used in conjunction with another to form a whole new word and meaning. It takes some time, but I can usually figure them out."

She smiled at him. He was so smart and cunning. Gentle and kind. He challenged her and broadened her mind in ways she never knew she could. Like learning runes. "Teach me some?" she asked.

He smiled, eyes bright and excited. "Of course."

After an hour of learning runes and even helping him decode a few for the crystal coffin, she only began to scratch the surface. It was so much more in-depth than she originally gave it credit for. But her mind was buzzing, and her stomach demanded food.

She excused herself with a kiss to his cheek and left him to continue his research so she could get some food. And once she had downed a bowl of spicy stew meat and vegetables, she stared at the hut wondering if Ezekiel was any closer to figuring out how to open the coffin than he was before.

"Eureka!" Ezekiel's voice carried through the village to Sophia, making her heart lurch forward, and she jumped up and ran to him.

"I found the key! It was as I suspected. The scroll and the runes on the base of the coffin coincide with each other."

Relief flooded through her and she went to gather Andreas and Edric. Once everyone was there, they surrounded the coffin, and Ezekiel made the final preparations to the potion that would help Madison wake up and heal.

~

EZEKIEL

Ezekiel nodded to himself. The potion prepared from the herbs was finally ready. He sat it down next to the coffin and then made the necessary markings on the crystal. He paused to think back to his training at the academy, at what he was taught about potion-making and how he was going to apply that to this situation. Normally, potions were designed for specific things. Individual things. This potion was created with the purpose of waking up and healing. But the herbs were so powerful and very volatile.

The extreme concentration he had to keep while making the potion was of utmost importance. Too much of one ingredient and not enough of the other would tip the purpose of this particular potion from healing and restoration to damage and disintegration.

But he was confident he had done everything correctly, even going as far as to sample a drop of the potion himself before committing it to the heir. With the desired effects coursing through his veins, he knew he had done everything correctly.

Now he just needed to make sure he had the runes to handle.

Pausing to double check his work in his notebook, he ensured that everything was correct and focused himself.

Now was the time to utter the words. There was no room for mistake. One single syllable mispronounced could spell the end of the heir and Sophia's destiny.

He pulled in a deep breath through his nose and let it out through his pursed lips.

He infused the runes along the crystal with his magic and whispered the incantation. Only a couple of words.

The runes started to glow and glimmer, brightening as light edged its way along the base of the coffin, to the sides, and along to the top and the crease. The crystal started to crack, and Ezekiel's breath caught.

Did I make a mistake? Did I kill the queen? He kept his questions to himself and continued to maintain his focus, despite the fear that he screwed everything up.

More cracks and the seal along the coffin broke open, parting into a slight opening.

Sophia, Edric, and Andreas removed the top.

Everyone stared at the heir, not moving. Not breathing.

Ezekiel picked up the potion and gently lifted Madison's head so that he could gently pour in small amounts of the liquid into her mouth. He poured a little liquid into her slightly parted lips and waited a few moments before adding more. He knew the liquid would have to drain down her throat, and he didn't want to make a mess over the front of her or have the liquid seep into the wrong hole.

As soon as the last of the liquid was poured into her mouth, he waited a few moments before laying her head back on the pillow underneath her.

And they waited.

Slowly, almost undetectable at first, her skin held a bit more color. Her hair became more vibrant. Her lips parted and her chest raised as she took in a deep breath.

Everyone sighed in relief at the same time. Ezekiel was sure each of them silently thanked the gods for this working as well. He certainly did. His heart could now return to its normal pace and position instead of fluttering in his throat.

Madison's eyelids twitched and opened. She instantly found Sophia and smiled.

"Hello cousin," she said in a full, rich voice that hadn't been affected by the years of sleep.

Ezekiel became puzzled by her term of endearment toward Sophia. Cousin?

"I'm glad to see you are well," she said. "But you look so much older."

CHAPTER TWENTY-ONE

"*C*ousin?" Sophia asked. She couldn't believe that she had found part of her family. And for the heir to recognize and address her directly threw her through a loop. Was she supposed to bow? Say Your Majesty or Highness?

She was completely out of her element and didn't know what to do.

Madison smiled radiantly and said, "Yes. Don't you recognize me?" She moved to sit up and Ezekiel quickly steadied her, helping her to sit fully after over a decade of lying flat.

"Much has changed in your absence, Your Majesty," Edric said.

She turned her blue eyes toward him and nodded. There was a sadness in that gaze that Sophia could relate to.

Ezekiel said, "How about we help you out of this coffin and get you some different clothing?"

"That would be wonderful. Thank you," Madison said and held her hand out perfectly poised, as Sophia always thought royalty did.

"I'll grab the clothing from one of the wraith's daughters," Andreas said and left the hut.

"I'll grab some food and water," Edric said, and left to do so.

After Sophia and Ezekiel successfully removed Madison from the coffin and helped her sit on a bench dragged in from outside, Ezekiel excused himself to allow Sophia and her newfound cousin to catch up.

But Sophia couldn't stop staring to get her thoughts in order. All this time, she knew she had family *somewhere* out there, she just never imagined "family" was the heir to the Nighthelm throne. There were similarities, sure. Like the blue eyes and blond hair. But her smile was as bright as the sun's and she was beautiful.

She had so many questions about her past. So many things she had always longed to say to her family once she found them. Many, many things. But her thoughts were so jumbled and chaotic, she couldn't form a single syllable much less an entire sentence.

Madison adjusted the gown over her legs and smiled at Sophia. "I'm so glad to see you well."

Sophia blinked her daze away and swallowed the lump in her throat. Her mouth went dry. She cleared her throat and said, "And I'm so glad to have found you."

"What has happened since I've been..." she looked to the crystal coffin. A flash of sadness washed over her expression. It was gone just as quick as it had showed. "Away."

Sophia nodded. "I was trained by Professor Grindel and Headmistress Mittle as a fighter. I didn't know what my purpose was. As an *anima contritum*, I was kept hidden and away from the eyes of Nighthelm. I spent my days training and nights patrolling Witch Woods, keeping the city safe, and... well, wishing for a day when I could live around people."

"Your soul was broken?" Madison asked. Her voice cracked and her words were filled with sadness and something else Sophia couldn't quite place.

The memory of her soul being broken flashed through her mind. Sophia frowned, and staring at a clump of dirt on the floor, she nodded. "It was when the vexsnare attacked you."

Her voice sounded different, almost distant, to her own ears.

Madison shifted and landed on her knees right in front of Sophia. Before she could ask what was wrong, the heir wrapped her arms around Sophia in a tight hug. "I'm so sorry cousin. You must have gone through nightmares and horrific torture to have endured that."

Sophia slowly wrapped her arms around her cousin and breathed in the soft rose petal scent of her hair. She smelled like family. Like home. A place she had only dreamed of but never thought she truly had.

"I promise to bring justice to you," Madison said.

"It's my job to protect you, Cousin," Sophia softly said against Madison's blond hair.

She pulled away, sitting regally on her knees and leveled her deep blue gaze on Sophia. "We're family, and we only have each other left. Once I'm queen, I will make sure no one can harm you again."

Her words were firm and offered no room for argument. Sophia wasn't used to that. With her men, maybe. And even then, that was difficult to get used to. But this was her cousin, the heir to Nighthelm, and she wasn't about to start arguing with her now. In Sophia's mind, Madison was already queen. And what the queen says, goes. No questions. No arguments.

Sophia softly smiled and took her cousin's hands into her own. "Thank you."

Madison smiled, ever radiant. "Of course. So, continue your story."

"I grew up not remembering anything of my past, though I had a feeling my teachers knew more than they let on. When I turned eighteen, I stood before the oracles and they gave me a quest to find the missing pieces of my soul and restore the heir to the throne."

"Were they working for someone else?" Madison asked. "Your teachers?"

Sophia said, "Yes. The Nameless Master. No one knows who he really is."

"That will be one of the first things I do as queen then." Madison nodded and shifted to sit on her rear.

"I found you in that coffin in a cave within Ripthorn. As soon as I saw the painting of your mother, father, and, I assume, sister?"

"Yes," Madison said and forced back the tears by pressing the heel of her hand into her eyes.

"I knew you were the heir. I had to save you. Zeke helped with his amazing ability to decipher runes. He's one of the top sorcerers of Nighthelm. Or he was until they all were labeled as traitors for associating with me."

Madison's lips pressed into a thin line. "Who is in charge?"

"Duchess Anabel Tryst. The steward," Sophia said.

"That woman has no business being on my throne. She will be punished, Cousin. That, I assure you."

"In time, Madison. I promise."

"You have grown so much," she said, cupping her cheek. "I still remember the day you came to live with us. Your parents were killed. I don't know under what circumstance, but you were proud and strong, even then."

"Who were they?" Sophia asked, curious to learn more about her mysterious past.

"I can only tell you, your last name is Delmonte. A prominent name in Ripthorn. That is all I know."

Sophia nodded. "Thank you. As soon as you are well enough, we will go to Nighthelm and restore you to the throne. Then you can be free to take care of all those that had harmed our family."

She sat straighter. "I'm well enough now."

"You just woke up, Cousin," Sophia said. She was a little surprised that the heir was so strong already. She had just woken from a sleep that lasted longer than a decade. And even then, Sophia almost ran out of time to save her. That potion that Ezekiel had made must have done a lot more than just heal and wake her.

"Be that as it may, I am renewed and wish to see order restored in my kingdom."

Sophia sat in awe, marveling at the strength her cousin had. She could understand Madison's desire to set things right. That had been her own motivation for quite some time. To serve and protect and belong. Right the wrongs.

Madison and Sophia continued with their discussion. Sophia explained who her men were and what they had gone through to get Madison healed and out of the coffin. With each event Sophia explained,

Madison nodded, eyes focused and formulating a plan. She wanted to ask about the thoughts she could see clearly passing through her cousin's gaze, but assured herself that in time, her cousin would share what she needed to.

Her cousin moved and held herself with such strength and poise that it was hard to believe she had just been so close to death just a couple hours ago. Had Sophia not been around to observe the event in its entirety, she wouldn't believe a moment of it. But she was there. And the sight astounded her.

Edric and Andreas returned with food, drink, and fresh clothing. Madison graciously thanked them and took her time eating at the behest of Ezekiel, who worried about the effects of food after such a long time without it and wanted to ensure she didn't make herself sick.

Once she finished eating, Sophia and her men stepped out of the hut to give Madison privacy to change. As soon as she stepped out and joined Sophia and her men, Madison looked ready for battle. Her hair was tied back in a braid, which fell past her shoulders and was secured with a leather lace.

She stood proud and tall, and once everyone turned toward her, knees were bent.

A collective of voices chanted, "All hail the queen!" Her gaze swept across all of them. She paused a little longer on Sophia, and she could tell her cousin was grateful for all of them. Her eyes watered, and her nostrils flared as she took in a deep breath.

"Ten years ago," Madison said, "I was running for my life with my cousin, Sophia. My little sister had died in the attacks that took your king and queen. I will take care of the usurpers that destroyed my family and home once I take back the throne that was stolen from my family."

Cheers erupted. The crowd of wraiths chanted again as Sophia, Edric, Andreas, and Ezekiel joined Madison.

"With all respect, Your Highness," Edric said. "Getting back into Nighthelm will be difficult."

"I'm aware of the issues, Commander. Sophia filled me in. But there is a passage only royalty could use. That was the same one we took when we escaped to the mountain. I will lead us through there, and we will kill the duchess for her mutiny and audacity to assume the throne."

Andreas said, "I assume there is so much more to all the events that have taken place. The duchess doesn't have the power or experience necessary to take the throne on her own. She had to have had help."

Ezekiel said, "I agree."

"We first need to restore my cousin to the throne, then we can all find the answers needed," Sophia said.

Madison nodded.

"We should be ready for a fight," Edric said. "We'll also need to protect Her Highness."

"My brothers will join us," Andreas said. He looked to Mica and Ozul. They nodded and started rounding up more wraiths.

"First," Edric said, "we should rest until a few hours before dawn. Then, under the cover of shadows, we'll make our move."

"Agreed," Madison said, though Sophia knew if they left that moment, it would make her all the happier. But it was a smart decision to wait until after nightfall.

With the plan set, and arrangements being made to gather more wraiths, Sophia could rest assured her destiny was nearly complete. All that was left was getting Madison on the throne, and something inside Sophia knew the fight had only just begun.

CHAPTER TWENTY-TWO

SOPHIA

*S*ophia knew she needed to rest, but part of her wanted to ask Madison more questions about her past and their family. She tried to keep that desire at bay by reminding herself that once Madison was on the throne, she would have time to learn all she could about the past that she had forgotten. Restoring the heir was top priority, so she needed to rest in order to be at her best.

Still, she slept lightly.

Once the time came to get up and make their move, she barely contained her excitement.

This was it.

This was her destiny, and she was oh so close to fulfilling it.

Unwilling to take the risk of the wrong people recognizing Madison, Sophia and her men made sure to disguise her and kept her at the center of the wraiths. She blended in well with the clothing she borrowed. It should work effortlessly.

Ezekiel and Andreas took up the back of the group, while Sophia and Edric took the front. And as they made their way back to the walls of Nighthelm, every eye raked the shadows for any hint of the grimms. They were still after Sophia for killing one of their own, and the last thing anyone needed was for Madison to be fatally wounded by one of the creatures when she was so close to claiming the throne.

But after what seemed like a few close calls for Sophia's taste—growls and roars that seemed to have followed them from the village—they arrived at the walls, unscathed and without event.

"There is a hidden passage where the mountain meets the castle. It should be hidden, and a bit overgrown by now," Madison said.

Sophia nodded at Edric as she met his gaze then stepped as silent as a ghost toward the wall of the castle at the back, where the mountain met the castle. At first, Sophia couldn't see anything. She looked over her shoulder at her cousin, who nodded once, urging her to continue.

She did and went to a large boulder near the rockface of the mountain. She studied it for a moment then walked around the side. There was a tunnel. With Edric by her side, she led her group into the tunnel that was extremely old, with cracks along the walls, and in disuse, but they made it through with little issue.

This whole time Sophia expected... something. A trap. A few Nighthelm guards. Anything that would line up the way damn near every trip into Nighthelm had. This time was easy. Too easy. And that put Sophia on edge more than the anticipation of something or someone making their trip difficult.

By the time they made it inside the castle and its lower halls, that feeling had increased. Sophia felt twitchy. Her heart hammered in her chest and she knew more than ever that something was amiss.

"Something's not right," she whispered to Edric.

He nodded and said, keeping his voice low as well, "Stay alert."

"Go right," Madison said, voice soft but carried enough for Sophia to hear.

She turned at the intersection.

After a few more directions from Madison, Sophia started to think they were in the clear. She wondered if that was because they had Madison with them. The castle would recognize its true ruler and aim to protect her. It made sense. Especially after all the stories she had heard about the castle's abilities and innate magic that was meant to protect the rulers.

She took one step forward.

Alarms sounded and traps in the halls triggered. Nighthelm guard rushed behind the group.

Sophia rolled her shoulders and pulled on her sword and dagger. It had been a trap all along. She whispered, "*Vocavi.*"

Haris's image evaporated into mist from her arm, swelling and growing until he solidified next to her. He stomped his feet and nodded his head up and down, seeming agitated and itching to get this fight done and over with.

She patted her friend's flank and said, "One more fight, my friend, and we'll have the heir restored."

He trilled and shook his head. A groan rumbled in his throat and he dashed forward.

"Protect the heir!" Sophia shouted and rushed into the fight.

Wraiths surrounding Madison shifted and cloaked her in shadow while others rushed forward to take out the guards that would sooner kill everyone, blindly following the orders of the duchess rather than using their brains. The guards wouldn't listen to reason or believe Madison was the true heir to the throne.

All at once, spears shot down from the ceiling, jutted from the walls, and poked up from the floors, right as Sophia was about to step into them. She shifted her weight and slid along her thigh and rotated to stop before getting skewered. They seemed like they were on a timer, with an impossible window to get through before becoming a kabob.

She took a few steps back as grunts and screams echoed from behind her. The castle seemed like it was throwing everything it had at the group.

Risking a glance behind her, a few squares of floor opened up and some fire traps had caught a few wraiths. She cursed under her breath. They had to move. They couldn't risk harm to Madison. She knew it was only a matter of time before someone triggered a trap over the very spot the heir stood. If she didn't figure out a way out of this mess before then, the whole mission would be for naught.

Sophia conjured a ball of light and studied the spears that shot out simultaneously directly in front of her. They were metal and stone and wood. If she could time it right, perhaps she could break them with her sword. The guards on the other side of the traps held out crossbows.

Of course, this would get much more difficult.

Magic bubbled just beneath the surface of her skin. She kept it down. The last thing she wanted was to incinerate Madison in an effort to take down the guards. Though she felt more confident about having control over her magic, she didn't want anything to happen to the heir before she could reclaim her birthright.

But maybe…

A plan formulated in her mind. If she could direct her magic, instead of letting it out in all directions, perhaps she could focus it outward and take out the trap and the guards.

It was a risk. She just wasn't sure it was a risk worth taking. And time ran short.

She turned to the wraiths. "Protect the queen. I'm going to try something."

"What are you doing?" Edric asked.

"Saving our lives," she said. "Hopefully."

She pulled on her magic, it pooled in her belly and she felt it pulsing through her arms. She steadied her hands, extending them in the direction of the trap and guards.

"Get behind me," she said as she held up her arms. They began to glow and spark with blue, purple, and white.

She took in a deep breath and kept her focus.

A dart flew past her, catching on her arm. Sharp, stinging pain throbbed as her sleeve soaked up the blood. Luckily, the dart clattered to the ground after hitting her arm and the wall just beside her.

Refocusing, she lifted her arms and held her hands toward the guards. With a battle cry, she released her magic. A blast of heat burst from her palms and shot forward. The force knocked her back a few feet, ending with her on her back. She quickly scrambled to her feet and checked that none of the men were hurt, and more importantly, Madison.

"That was amazing, Cousin!" she said as her eyes met Sophia's.

Her men were fine.

The trap and the guards, however, weren't. And without missing a beat, she rushed down the hall, keeping her ears trained on any sound outside of footsteps and her eyes alert to any movement.

She wasn't sure how many more traps she could take out with her magic. She used the sword for any others that could be disarmed, and her and her men took out any guards that stepped in their way.

As they fought, they inched closer to the main floor of the castle. The closer they got, the more traps and guards they had to fight through.

When they finally reached the door to the main floor, the group paused to catch their breath. There was no telling what they would find beyond the door. It could be empty. Or, it could be filled with the remaining city guard.

Either way, they needed to collect themselves.

"Everyone all right?" she asked.

A few grunts and groans, but for the most part, they hadn't endured a loss in their numbers.

She nodded and placed her hand on the handle of the door. Twisting it, the door clicked and opened an inch.

Now or never.

She stepped through and stopped as her eyes focused on the second of the possibilities. The guard stood at attention, weapons poised and aimed straight at her.

CHAPTER TWENTY-THREE

SOPHIA

*W*ho would ever think returning the heir to the throne would be such a pain in the ass? Particularly for Sophia.

She was winded, but still stood strong, especially with her magic. She had repeated her little tactic from the halls beneath the castle, and each time she had better results. But it seemed like the more guards she took out, more of them would appear.

Haris remained in the shadows, picking off the guards that got too close. His movements were quick and fluid, and because of his size, he easily toppled a few guards or knocked them back. He seemed as strong as ever.

Sophia looked for her men. They took off with the group of wraiths not guarding Madison and headed in all directions to take out the guard. She couldn't see them.

A guard approached and nearly took her head off with his sword. She ducked in the nick of time and parried with an attack of her own. But he was strong, and with each one of his attacks, she was pushed farther back, toward a wall.

She tried to gain more ground, pushing him back a step with her attacks, but the effort seemed useless. Her boot stomped on a stone behind her and the castle started to shift.

Another trap.

Before she had time to realize what was happening, it was too late. She had been separated from her men and Madison. She knew the men were more than capable of holding their own and would stop at nothing to make sure Madison remained unharmed.

She was capable as well. And if it was the last thing she did, she would knock that undeserved crown from the duchess's head. Smile and all.

Jumping into action, she ran down the halls, searching for the woman. She had a vague idea of where the throne room was and assumed, if she were the duchess, that was where she would be. Sitting all high and mighty in a seat she didn't belong in and acting proud of her efforts to bring the monster of Nighthelm to justice.

With a few disarmed traps and a couple of dead

guards later, Sophia made it to the throne room. She paused to catch her breath. Her heart pounded wildly in her chest.

As she stepped in as casually as she could, her eyes shifted to the throne where the duchess unsurprisingly sat.

The image of that woman being in her cousin's seat fueled Sophia's anger, as well as her energy and strength.

The duchess angled her gaze at her, looking down at Sophia from the bridge of her nose. Her aunt's crown sitting upon the woman's head.

Bitterness filled Sophia's mouth like poison.

This woman had the audacity to kill Sophia's family for the throne. She nearly succeeded in killing her and her men. But the bitch's reign ended tonight.

Sophia held her sword out, tip of the blade pointed at the duchess's heart. "You have no right to sit there."

The duchess laughed and clapped her ring covered hands. "I have more right than a little *contritum* like you."

"Less right than Madison," Sophia said.

The duchess rolled her eyes. "You are a constant pain in the ass. Still, though, you are of use to me. As my slave, you will serve me and remain in my power."

"Fat fucking chance," she said. Sophia's anger churned within her veins, boiling and bubbling, making her magic rise. She quickly took in a deep breath realizing that the duchess was trying to get her to lose control.

She began wondering why the duchess wanted her to lash out, and why she wasn't afraid if she did. Sophia's gaze quickly swept across the throne room, just in case the duchess had some sort of trap or surprise. She stared at the woman, holding on to her magic and forcing herself to calm down. Her next move would have to be a calculated one.

The duchess shifted on the throne, straightening her back. "I intended to break your soul or end your life. Just like I killed your precious family. No thanks to Winston for fucking up my original plans."

"For what? Power?"

The duchess smiled. "Oh no, my dear, for so much *more* than power. But I don't owe you any explanation. My plans are my own and have worked for the better part of a decade. Until you came along and started shoving your nose into business it didn't belong in."

"Perhaps. But the only reason why you are caught is because I was smarter than you," Sophia said, keeping her sword trained on the duchess, never letting the woman see her waiver. Not even a little.

"You will never take this crown from me." The woman sneered. "I shouldn't have even let you live. But that magic would've been wasted. I couldn't let that happen. No, it doesn't matter anymore. Even if you were to take this throne from me, the people will never accept you or your so-called heir. The monster I turned you into will make you hated forever."

"You have already lost the people," Sophia said, her voice echoing through the room. "They have already cheered my name. Which you would know if you weren't so preoccupied with stealing a seat that wasn't yours to begin with."

"Ha! One simple event doesn't free you of who you are." The duchess stood. "You are a monster, a broken, little thing. You don't even know what happened to you, do you? Your mind is as jumbled as a child's puzzle. If you do not submit to me, now, then you'll never learn the truth of what happened to your parents."

For a moment, the comment stung her. More than anything she wanted to regain her memory and understand more about her family, especially since she found Madison. However, the duchess had proven herself untrustworthy and manipulative. A murderer. Usurper. Her words would have to be carefully sifted through, and even then they would be worth little. No, Sophia would find out the truth, and her beloved men would help her, along with Madison—the true queen of Nighthelm.

Sophia saw through the duchess and refused to let the woman manipulate her feelings. She knew everything she needed to know, and she would see to it that the duchess got her just desserts. She would die to make sure her cousin got the throne back. Madison was the rightful queen. Not this pretender.

As the duchess approached Sophia, her amulet around her neck started to glow. "You are going to join your family. As soon as you watch me murder your cousin, I'll make you suffer a long, torturous death."

Bells sounded outside of the castle, mixed with growls and the cries of the people. They echoed around her, and she couldn't contain her anger anymore.

CHAPTER TWENTY-FOUR

ANDREAS

*A*ndreas knew the second the castle had shifted that he, his brothers, and men were separated from Sophia.

Luckily, Madison had remained with them and safe. A few of the wraiths surrounding her joined the fight at moments when he and his brothers were nearly overwhelmed with the sheer onslaught of guards fighting against them.

He could only guess how Edric was holding up, forced to kill the very men he once led. Andreas quickly searched for him between fighting guards. He had just taken down another one, met Andreas's gaze, and shouted, "Keep fighting! We must stand for the rightful queen!"

His wraith brothers roared, filling his blood with pride. Edric, ever the commander, knew just what to say to keep the group motivated. He was destined for leadership. Bred for it, even.

Andreas shouted, "For the queen!" and shifted.

He quickly checked on Madison again and started taking out guards, tasting their fear and rushing to them before they could get a chance to do the same to him. Though it was a bloodied fight, having endured some injuries of his own, he knew in the end, Madison would take over the duchess's position and become queen. Her birthright.

"This is what we fight for!" he shouted again, aiding Edric in keeping the fight going strong even though he knew strength was ebbing.

They needed to get Madison to the throne room. Then they could rest. He knew Sophia was safe. It almost seemed like there was nothing that could hold that woman back. He chuckled to himself. That woman of his. He never could get enough of her. She was the only one who ever looked at him from the start and truly saw him. A person. Not a monster.

Edric's voice called out, "Your queen stands before you. Stop fighting us and see her reclaim the throne."

"Lies," one guard said. "You're under the spell of that *contritum* woman. Nothing you say is truth."

"But it is true, brothers. Sophia has done no harm," he said. "Look at the girl, she is your true queen."

Madison stood a little taller, even though her eyes were wide with fear. This was probably the same sight she had seen just before being put into that crystal coffin. Andreas felt for her. He didn't want to see any more death himself. After what she had been through, he couldn't blame her for being afraid.

"Mockery," another guard said, aiming his pike at the group.

Andreas said, "We are of our own free will. Let us pass and end this bloodshed so that we may prove her right and claim to the throne."

Though a few of the guard seemed to see reason in his and Edric's words, he knew by the way their gazes darted between them and their comrades, they wouldn't dare turn on their group. They were banded together.

"Blasphemy." The insult came as an echo among some of the other guards.

Andreas sighed. It seemed like it would take much more to prove Madison was the rightful heir, more than just words. They were too far under the power and corruption of the duchess to even entertain his and his brothers' claims. They barely held a human look in their eyes.

Ezekiel stepped in front of Andreas as he turned to face off with another guard. He took him down with a blast of fire and then ice. "They're not listening. We need to get Madison to the throne room." He didn't so much as blink before rushing off to take care of another.

As he passed the carnage, the damaged walls and torn tapestries that once hung across them, he knew by the end of this fight that they would need to do considerable repairs to the castle. He was sorry Madison's arrival had to be amidst a battle, but the duchess and her forces left them no choice.

But before any of them could work on rebuilding, everyone needed to be healed, of course. His own body ached from blows landed and his arms stung from cuts endured.

Despite the damage done to the castle, the important thing was keeping Madison safe as they made their way to the throne room. Even with some of the most severe close calls Andreas had dodged, he managed to hold his own.

He just hoped he could keep up the momentum until the throne room.

CHAPTER TWENTY-FIVE

SOPHIA

*T*he duchess reached Sophia on the main floor of the throne room and paced a circle around her. Sophia kept up with her, never taking her eyes off the woman for one bloody second.

The woman walked to a nearby wall and pulled off a ceremonial sword that had once belonged to one of Sophia's ancestors. She paused to examine the blade and said, "Did you know, child, that even ceremonial blades are kept sharp?"

Sophia didn't answer.

The duchess smiled as she angled her gaze down the blade and swiped it through the air a few times. Sophia thought she was showing off.

Big deal. You can swing a sword.

Hu-fucking-zah.

Sophia was far from impressed. She just wanted to

get the fight going already. All that talk about killing her and the damned woman wanted to show off a bit of basic skill? She shook her head.

The true test of skill would be in how she wielded the weapon and stood against Sophia.

The duchess shifted her gaze to Sophia. "Once I defeat you, I'll have you chained until that heir is captured. Then I'll execute her right in front of you. You'll break completely and submit to my control, or I will kill you."

"A lot of talk for someone with a plan of action. Stalling doesn't suit you," Sophia said and held her position against the duchess.

"Smarting off to your master isn't wise," the woman said. "Guess I'll have to teach you a lesson as well."

Sophia snorted. "How to talk someone to death?"

The woman leveled her cold, hardened gaze on hers and said, "No dear, to respect your elders."

She attacked with amazing fierceness and strength. It surprised Sophia that the woman actually knew how to handle and use a blade. No matter. They were more evenly matched now, and that gave Sophia an advantage. An inexperienced fighter was unpredictable and more dangerous than experienced fighters at times. Now, she could gauge the woman's movements and predict where the next attack would come from.

Sophia blocked the next blow and parried. She felt a little stronger, urged to continue.

The cries from the citizens continued and grew louder, getting closer to the castle. So were the growls and howls of the grimms.

She needed to get this fight done and over so she could take care of the damned creatures. She wondered why the grimms charged into the city. Now, of all times. But before she could figure that out, the duchess swiped her blade toward Sophia's midsection, forcing her to jump back or get sliced open.

She glared at the woman and fought even harder, attacking stronger, with more vigor and determination than the last blow.

It wasn't long before she could see the duchess weakening, becoming winded. Apparently, no one taught her how to breathe when fighting. Even though she only looked slightly drained, Sophia needed to end this woman. If only she could nail a deadly blow.

Despite her appearance, the duchess was skilled and able to deflect each attack, parrying with a blow of her own which continued to surprise Sophia since the woman always seemed so frail. Yet, she fought like a hardened warrior.

Sophia needed to up the tactics and her own defenses if she had any hope of defeating the woman. She called on her magic, pooling inside her and waiting to be let loose.

After the next parry, she threw her fist out. A blast of light shot from her hand. The duchess quickly ducked out of the way and the blow hit the stone wall on the far side of the throne room.

The duchess smirked and held her sword at the ready. "You'll have to do better than that, dear."

Sophia groaned inwardly. This woman was baiting her, trying to trick her into losing control over her magic so she could win and get the people on her side again. All her efforts of restoring Madison to the throne would be lost and the duchess would likely succeed in killing off the last remaining heir of Nighthelm.

Over my dead body.

And that's exactly what it would take for the duchess to succeed. But failing wasn't an option Sophia would accept, and she fought harder. Used her magic more. And before long, the throne room was a mess of disintegrated stone.

If she didn't end this fight soon, there wouldn't be a throne left for Madison to sit on much less a stable room.

Still, Sophia didn't lose focus. She was taking her life, freedom, and her cousin's throne back. She was taking her family back. The duchess held too much control over her and the people of Nighthelm for too long, and Sophia wanted to make sure the woman couldn't hurt another person. Never again.

With a feigned attack to the left, Sophia used her sword and stabbed the duchess's side. She cried out as her knees nearly gave from under her. Blood seeped through her well-fitting, expensive dress. But the woman seemed more angered by the cut and glared at Sophia.

The duchess reached for the amulet, glowing even brighter.

Smoke seeped from her pores and shadows seemed to grow around her.

Her form started to shift and grow, melting and darkening to black. The shadows covered her body, creating a shroud. Her hands thinned and turned boney and frail. The mist surrounded her like a fog, and when it was all over, the Nameless Master stood before Sophia.

She took a step back to process what she just saw and couldn't bring herself to make sense of the corruption of the duchess's soul for the number of times she had to have taken the form of the Nameless Master.

Bright lights erupted all around Sophia as images sprang to life in blips and flashes. Her world faded until she was consumed by the memories. By the truth of what happened all those years ago.

Running.

Pain.

Fear.

She and Madison ran side by side, hand in hand through the halls in the belly of the castle. Madison—this girl was family. A sister.

No, that's not right...

Cousin.

Sophia had no sister, no family but Madison and her parents, the king and queen. They adopted her. In the depths of the memory, where emotion blurred with the walls, skewing reality, Sophia could only remember that her parents were dead, long dead, at this point. There was no home anymore, no sense of family but Madison. Besides the halls of Nighthelm, Sophia had nowhere else to go.

Now, she was faced with more loss and running for her life.

Behind them, grimms charged through the halls. Screams of children and adults alike echoed around her, propelling her forward, fueling the fires of her terror. Screams would end abruptly, or with a guttural moan, and she knew she had to keep running to stay alive. The grimms were here for her. For Madison. Anyone who hid them, anyone who stood in the way would die.

And she would be next.

Madison pulled on her hand, tugging hard as they fled to keep her as close as possible. "We have a friend waiting for us," she said, panicked and out of breath. "He will take us to safety."

Another little girl grabbed Sophia's hand, and she knew it was her friend from the kitchens. Sophia loved going there and playing with the little girl. She considered her a sister as well.

But the grimms had caught up and the little girl was gone. She still couldn't remember the name of the child, but they were close, and her face was as familiar as family.

They ran until her legs ached and her lungs burned. They had entered a tunnel in the mountain and encountered a vexsnare. Covered in blood, they couldn't hide from him. Madison tucked Sophia into a small hole in the side of a wall and sealed it with a small boulder.

With tears streaming down her face, Sophia watched the shadows on the walls move as Madison screamed. Grimms and a vexsnare.

The screaming stopped. And there was so much blood covering the walls. Sophia couldn't hold in her sobs any longer. Something inside her heart broke. Inside her soul. Everything burned and numbed, and though her insides were ravished with fire, her skin felt like it was covered in ice.

That's when the Nameless Master found her.

But instead of killing her, the woman said in her gravely, raspy voice. "I may have use for you yet. Come along, child."

The images around her imploded into shimmering

dust that cascaded around her and the Nameless Master.

"You... You killed my family!" Sophia growled out the words. Rage and magic boiled beneath her skin, ravishing her nerves, begging to be released. But that was what the Nameless Master wanted. For her to lose control over herself. To prove she was nothing but an *anima contritum*. A thing that was too dangerous to live unless controlled by her.

The Nameless Master attacked in response.

Sophia blocked and parried, arms growing tired from the constant fighting. But the attacks kept coming. If she didn't do something to tip the scales in her favor, she just may lose control of herself and end up causing a catastrophic eruption that could disintegrate what was left of the throne room at the very least. The entire castle at most.

And she couldn't do that.

She had to defeat the Nameless Master. Failure wasn't an option.

CHAPTER TWENTY-SIX

SOPHIA

*S*ophia cursed under her breath. As if fighting off half of Nighthelm's army and the duchess wasn't enough for one night, now she had to fight the Nameless Master.

Again.

Never mind figuring out how to declare her cousin as heir to the throne.

Everything seemed almost insurmountable. But even as she faced off foes with impossible odds stacked against her, she was strong and capable. Resolute, she squared her shoulders and aimed her sword at the creature. The duchess was beyond help. She was so desperate for power, she corrupted her very soul to become a creature of darkness and death.

She learned the first time they had fought that the Nameless Master was powerful and strong. But strength and power be damned. Sophia would defeat this woman if it took her very last breath to do so.

"You would stoop this low for control and power?" Sophia asked.

The Nameless Master responded in her grating voice, "I would stop at nothing to keep what I deserve."

"How can you say that? You don't deserve the throne. You have destroyed lives, families, and manipulated the city and the guard."

Sophia dodged another blow from the creature that used to be the duchess and was knocked back a few feet with the next attack.

"Yes," she said in her raspy voice. "I even broke you, ripped apart your soul. But you've outgrown your usefulness and become nothing but a pain in the ass. Now, I will finish you."

The Nameless Master released everything within her, attacking with vicious force. She fought without pause and no holds barred. Sophia struggled to keep up as she parried the strikes. She stepped wrong and got a nice slice of the blade along the left side of her torso. She hissed in response to the pain.

Sophia's muscles ached and her rapidly beating heart felt as if it were going to burst out of her chest. She drew in a deep breath and focused, knowing she was running out of steam. Things were looking grim.

The Nameless Master sensed Sophia's exhaustion, and she looked ready to deliver her final blow. Edric,

Ezekiel, and Andreas showed up with his wraith brothers. Madison stayed as far behind as she could, remaining covered by the wraiths surrounding her, keeping her safe.

Sophia returned her gaze to the Nameless Master. She tightened her grip on her weapon and leveled her sword at the woman. The odds had just turned in their favor.

Or so she thought.

The Nameless Master went around Sophia and charged right for Madison.

Oh no you don't.

Sophia ran toward Madison, slid on the side of her thigh, then pivoted to her knees and stood as the Nameless Master was in the middle of a downward stroke of her sword. Sophia's blade met with a blast of magic that tossed the Namless Master back on her ass.

"We're not done yet," she told the corrupted form of what used to be the Duchess of Westray.

The creature stood with what seemed like a growl. "When will you stop getting in the way of matters that don't concern you?"

"She's my family!"

Sophia attacked. The sword glowing with the magic within her. Despite the wound in her side causing her pain. The Nameless Master got in a few good shots with a slice across Sophia's thigh and a few nicks on her arms.

She couldn't get an edge over the creature.

Grimms rushed into the room. Growls and screams filled the air as Sophia continued to face off with the Nameless Master. She grew distracted, checking over her shoulder to make sure Madison was okay. Sharp claws scratched at Sophia's chest, snapping her attention back to the fight.

Two can play that game.

Sophia pulled on her dagger and used both it and her sword to fight the creature. Anger pulsed through her body as memories played through her mind. Sophia had a family once, a loving childhood that was destroyed be the duchess who craved power so deeply, she killed that family and broke her soul.

With each thought and memory, Sophia attacked a little harder.

With each memory, her heart broke a little more.

She forced back the tears and kept attacking a little quicker and harder, knocking the dark creature back toward a wall.

She worried for Madison and her men. Always trying to angle herself in a way she could observe through her periphery. But the Nameless Master used every instance to keep the attention on her.

"Kill them all!" The creature's voice burned Sophia's ears.

Was this it? Was this the moment her men died?

Could she save them and Madison and end this fight once and for all?

If Sophia had a say in it, no one would die before the duchess.

She kicked the woman back against the wall and held up the sword, glowing as bright as the sun and said, "Enough! I, Sophia Delmonte, niece to the king, declare my cousin, Madison Averell, rightful heir to the throne of Nighthelm. You, Duchess Anabelle Tryst, Steward of Nighthelm, will relinquish your hold on this kingdom or die."

"I will never surrender to you!" the raspy voice said.

Sophia leaned in closer, aiming the sword at the Nameless Master's chest where the blackened heart would be and prepared to shove the blade through, magic and all. Her attention shifted to the glowing amulet. There was something about that thing that pulled on the back of Sophia's mind. She made a connection.

The duchess didn't shift into the Nameless Master until after it had started to glow. The amulet had to be the source of the power. That had to be what gave her control over the grimms.

With a flick of her wrist, she angled the blade of her sword under the chain and pulled back, breaking it.

The amulet fell away. And the Nameless Master shifted back into the duchess.

Sophia stepped away as the raspy screams turned into more human ones. Her form melted to the woman, albeit visibly weakened, as she screamed and fell to her knees, hands clenched into tight fists and a vein popping out on her forehead.

"What have you done?" the woman screamed at Sophia.

"I took away the power you never should have had," she said, standing tall as she realized the fighting had stopped. Her men stepped up behind her.

"You wretched wench! I'll kill you if it's the last thing I do. I curse you!"

Sophia lifted an eyebrow. Part of her wanted to feel pity for the woman. She still didn't know what caused the duchess to act out in such away, harboring the corrupting power of the amulet and killing her family just for the position to rule over Nighthelm. But she couldn't afford pity for such a calloused, evil woman. She deserved death, but most importantly, her family deserved justice.

The woman raged on the floor then stood and rushed Sophia. Claws splayed out and aimed for her throat. Without hesitation, Sophia dug the dagger deep into the woman's chest.

The duchess's eyes grew wide and filled with the knowledge that her life was at its end. There would be no more corruption in the city. No more death by grimms. No more fearmongering for the people. Her legacy ended with her last breath.

As the duchess fell limp to the floor, blood mixing with the debris of the nearly destroyed throne room, silence settled like a thick blanket. Not so much as a breath could be heard. It was nearly deafening.

Sophia pulled the dagger from the woman's chest and stared at her lifeless body. She avenged her family, but it didn't seem like enough. When she turned, she froze.

The grimms stood watching her. Waiting as if to pounce and make good on the promise they gave not so long ago, when she killed one of them. Instead, the leader approached with his head bowed.

"You saved us." His voice made her skin crawl. "You earned our respect."

Sophia went for the amulet. She found it lying where she cut it from the Nameless Master's neck and picked it up. It no longer glowed red. No longer controlled the grimms. The Nameless Master would never again force them into her service—they were free.

She approached the leader and held out the amulet to them. "No one deserves slavery."

He took the amulet, nodded, then left with his pack.

"That was..." Edric said, pulling Sophia's attention

to him. He shook his head, seemingly just as much at a loss of words as she was.

Madison approached, and Sophia asked, "Are you hurt?"

She shook her head. "I'm well, Cousin."

Sophia turned to her men, all of them having endured injuries of their own. Each one of them nodded. Sophia smiled, grateful each of them were still alive.

"Now what?" Andreas asked.

Sophia's smile grew wider. "We make Madison queen."

CHAPTER TWENTY-SEVEN

SOPHIA

*S*ophia stood in front of the oracles with her men and cousin behind her. Haris paced the garden around the trees, sniffing and swishing his tail. He seemed rather relaxed, which eased her nerves. With the sword of her family and the dagger from Grindel strapped to her belt, she knelt before the great trees, reverent as ever.

They awakened as an aura surrounded them. Their glowing eyes opened, and they focused on her.

"Little bird, why do you wake us?" The voices were in unison and vibrated over her much like it had before.

"To let you know I have done what you have asked of me. I found the heir, myself, and my soul. I did these things with your help, and I wanted to thank you."

Great work, you have done.
The throne is restored.
Though your purpose is not yet complete.
Through your destiny, dangers still lurk.
Enemies abound from mountain and air.
Still truth of history you must seek.
Others will come to undo the peace.
To attack the phoenix with foe and magic.
Take heed of the short days and longer nights.
Then you may rest your sword.

The glow around the oracles faded as they returned to their sleep.

"Well, it's always good to know more adventure and danger awaits us," Andreas said, clapping his hands together and rubbing them with a goofy grin.

Sophia chuckled, hoping that at least they'd be able to enjoy a respite before the next adventure began. "Let's get back to the castle. We have a queen to crown."

As they departed from the oracles and headed for the castle, a dull roar hit Sophia's ears. It was the people. Word had gotten out about what happened, and they quickly gathered to see for themselves. They chanted to see their queen, but the Nighthelm guard still didn't believe Madison was the true heir, much less the daughter of the king.

Sophia sighed. It seemed like there was more work to be done in the city after all.

They entered the town's center and Madison placed a hand on Sophia's arm to stop her. She turned to face her cousin. Madison smiled and said, "I'll talk to the people and settle this."

Reluctantly, Sophia nodded and handed her the sword. "You're going to need this."

"What for?"

"It is the sword of the kings," she said. "And it rightly belongs to you."

Madison seemed to think that over for a few moments then took the sword, clumsily hanging it on the belt of her dress. She stepped forward and addressed the people and her guard.

"People of Nighthelm, please be still and listen. I know you fear my cousin because of what she is and the rumors that brought about a certain reputation. However, she was not born this way. She was made. The duchess was not only responsible for the murder of my father, your king, but also for breaking my cousin's soul in an effort to turn her into a weapon to take over the kingdom for good.

"So nefarious was her plan, she was corrupted with dark magic and held the power of the Nameless Master.

"The duchess was also behind the ultimate downfall

of the royal family in an effort to take over and rule. Though we don't yet know why she had done such things, trust that as your rightful queen, I will do what I must to return this kingdom not only to its original glory but the peaceful times I was ever fond of as a child."

A guard stepped forward and said, "You say you are the queen? Prove it."

Sophia shifted her gaze to Edric who held the hilt of his sword with a frown. She knew it pained him to see his old comrades in arms acting in such a way. But no one could really blame them. They followed orders and were blindly loyal to the duchess. So much so, that they couldn't see the truth if it had bitten them in the ass.

Madison nodded. "Of course." She pulled on the sword at her side and held it up for all to see. "This is the sword of the kings, and only those who share of the same blood can safely wield it."

"That is just some hunk of metal," another guard said as he too stepped forward. "Anyone could find a fancy blade and claim it to be the sword of the kings."

Sophia frowned. They still weren't convinced.

The crowd grew even more unsettled.

"You prove you are the queen, or you will be killed for treason," another guard said.

Sophia's shoulders tightened with tension. Arrows and spears were aimed at her, her men, and Madison. The crowd erupted in boo's and shouts of disapproval.

Sophia dragged her gaze along the rows of guards, ready to take their heads at any moment. An arrow was loosed. She jumped in front of her cousin with her dagger drawn and magic sparking along her body.

A guard was reprimanded for releasing an arrow outside of command. He was a nervous sort. Which meant he was also dangerous. Sophia narrowed her eyes on the boy. If he was so inexperienced, he should've been given another duty. Thank the gods the arrow was poorly shot as well. Despite the arrow having been aimed at the queen, it hit only dirt and rock.

Andreas, Edric, and Ezekiel jumped in front of Sophia for her defense, and Haris jumped out from within the shadows in front of them.

Silence fell along the crowd as the people stared at the beast.

From behind them, a bright light burst forth.

Sophia faced Madison, who held the sword high, spreading its light all around them. Wind swirled around her body, billowing through her skirt and hair. Sophia smiled and stood in awe of her cousin. She stood so proud and strong. Humming sang from the blade, silencing only when she started to lower the sword.

A burst of energy thundered through the air, vibrating the buildings surrounding everyone and a bolt of lightning stuck the ground behind the group.

In its place stood a man. The same man Sophia saw in the painting.

King Duncan.

Reverent awes whispered through the crowd, and the guard replaced their weapons and bowed.

Madison rushed to her father and wrapped her arms tightly around the man.

He said, "I knew you would be the one to release me." He pulled away from his daughter to focus on Sophia. "Thank you for protecting the sword and bringing my daughter home."

Sophia nodded. As the king walked toward the crowd, she glanced at her cousin as she wiped away a tear from her cheek. Their gazes met, and Sophia smiled gently.

The king said, "My soul was trapped in the sword by a spell when I learned of the traitors and their intent to kill me and my family. Unfortunately, I learned too late how deep that treachery went."

Sophia took in a shuddering breath. She couldn't recall any memories of the man, but she knew him. His kind and gentle way. This was her uncle. Her lost family.

"I'm sorry for not being able to save my children and Sophia, but I rested peacefully knowing that my daughter would someday reclaim the throne and help set right what was wronged." He held his hand behind him. Madison rushed to take his hand and his side.

"I can now peacefully leave this realm and join the rest of my family in eternal slumber." Facing Madison once more, he said, "I am proud of you, and always will be. I know you will rule rightly and justly and bring prosperity to the kingdom once more."

Sophia swallowed the lump in her throat as she was once again reminded of the temptation the nymphs had offered. She hoped she could continue standing strong, in her uncle's name, and for the sake of her men.

King Duncan faced Sophia. "I'm proud of you as well Sophia and love you as much as I do Madison. You had to overcome so much to get here. You are strong and powerful. Your parents would be proud."

Sophia nodded as she blinked away tears, heart hammering in her chest. The validation she always craved and never once thought she would ever get just got delivered in the most spectacular way. And she was floored, awed by the presence of her uncle, and grateful for the kind words she never thought she would hear.

"You have amazed me with your undying loyalty and duty to the city. The test the nymphs gave you proved that you are selfless and courageous. I'm proud of you. You will need that strength and courage in the days to come."

"Thank you, Uncle."

He cupped his daughter's cheek and smiled before

taking a few steps away from both Madison and Sophia. As he moved, his form started to fade, losing physical opacity and becoming more ethereal until only an echo of his voice remained...

"Good bye, my children."

CHAPTER TWENTY-EIGHT

EDRIC

*E*dric stared in awe. His king, the man he looked up to all his life, stood right in front of him. In the flesh. Well, sort of. He took a knee with the rest of the city. The man was, after all, still Edric's King and Commander. Seeing him was a surreal experience.

When the king spoke, Edric listened to every syllable, every word, and even the inflection of his voice, as he spoke with pride and love toward not only his daughter, but Sophia as well. That man cared for his family like none other.

Edric held so much love and respect for his king that it tore at his heart to listen to the plot that led to his ultimate demise.

But even as the king spoke of such terrible things, the tension between the citizens and the guard was no longer. And now, even the guard couldn't argue Madison's claim.

Sophia would soon complete her destiny in restoring the heir to the throne. Even though he knew there was more to do. There was still more to set right, but he could rest easier knowing that, for now, things were going smoothly.

As the king disappeared, his heart panged for his loss. He admired that man and seeing him say goodbye was hard to endure.

Alarm settled in his nerves just as the king's final words faded. This was an all too familiar sensation. One that spoke of danger. Standing straight, Edric's eyes scanned the crowed and the shadows surrounding the buildings.

There.

Barely noticeable, but there was a figure in the shadows. Stealthy and dangerous. Had the person not moved just a fraction, he probably would've overlooked him.

Edric pulled on his sword and readied himself for whatever trouble there was to come.

CHAPTER TWENTY-NINE

SOPHIA

*S*ophia petted Haris's side and softly said, "Relax, boy."

But something told her it wasn't just the crowd and guard that had his hackles up. There was something she couldn't see. Sure, Haris had never truly revealed himself in front of such a large group before. That didn't excuse the immense sensation of danger lurking just out of sight.

Sophia could sense it.

Haris sensed it.

As her eyes shifted toward her men, she learned Edric sensed it too. His focus was on the crowd. He frowned, and his hand gripped the hilt of his sword.

Ezekiel's hands had a glow to them as he seemed focused on the same area as Edric.

An explosion of fire came from deep within the

crowd, aimed directly at her and Madison. The people rushed around, seeking cover and safety. Screams filled the air.

As she dodged the burning ball of flames, she knocked her cousin out of the way, taking the sword from her. Haris and her men leapt into action. She caught sight of a figure dressed in dark clothing, sticking to the shadows. It seemed humanoid in form, but she knew this was what the oracles had warned her of.

Another figure jumped in front of her, making a strike toward her. She dodged the blow of his sword by thrusting out her hand, pushing her own magic outward. He stumbled a few steps back, but quickly recovered. The buzzing sensation coursed through her and she felt the powerful sting of a blast pulsing through her.

No. I will not lose control.

The sword of the kings glowed and pulsed with radiant energy as she thrust the weapon into her attacker's stomach. She turned, ready for the next attack. This one held a double-bladed dagger in each hand. He swiped, cutting Sophia's forearm. She blocked the next attack, kicked him in the gut, and plunged her sword into his chest.

Sophia recognized the uniform from the assassins that attacked them in the mountain and in Witch Woods at the wraith village.

After taking out several more assassins, she faced the last with her men. Magic rippled over him, and he was readying for a spell that was sure to destroy this section of Nighthelm. Andreas, in wraith form, joined his side.

Haris growled as he inched closer to the assassin, head low as though he was getting ready to pounce on prey.

"Haris, Andreas, don't," Sophia said.

But all that did was bring the assassin's attention to her. He flung out his hand and a ball of lightning shot toward her. She instinctively held the sword in front of her, pushing her magic into it, creating a shield of light and warmth.

The ball hit, and the shield absorbed the power and force.

The assassin growled and said, "Why won't you die?"

Haris pounced, knocking the man to the ground.

"Don't kill him," Sophia said as she ran toward the attacker. Edric joined her at her side and held his sword pointed at the assassin's throat.

His hood fell back and revealed he was a lynx.

That's it. There definitely more behind those attacks than just common assassins from the mountain. And right now, the throne still sat empty. But Sophia had a feeling the attack was much more than a poor attempt at preventing Madison from becoming queen.

There was something so much deeper than that. Darker.

Edric asked, "Who sent you?" The tone of his voice made it sound more like a demand than a request.

The creature narrowed his gaze on Edric and said, "My queen will have her revenge!"

"Who is your queen?" Sophia asked.

He settled his steely eyes on her and moved to attack.

Edric shoved his sword into the creature's neck.

As the lynx choked and gargled blood that spewed from his mouth, he kept his glare focused on Sophia.

She wondered what had happened that caused such hate and eagerness to kill her. But now, she knew that it wasn't about the throne at all. It was about her.

CHAPTER THIRTY

EDRIC

*E*dric's blood boiled with the idea of someone trying to take his woman from him. Andreas, having shifted back to his human form, approached the body.

"He had been tortured to the point of being ugly," Andreas said and shook his head.

Edric didn't care what had happened to the creature during his life. He still tried to hurt Sophia. And that was something he wouldn't stand for.

Ezekiel looked down at the creature, standing near his head. "Why would creatures from the mountain want our Sophia dead?" He seemed genuinely puzzled.

"I'm afraid that would have to wait," an elder from the academy said. "The more pressing issue is getting the crown on the princess's head. Then we can worry about the attack."

Edric turned on the old man, point his sword at him. "How in the fuck is Madison getting crowned more important than someone trying to *kill* Sophia?"

The old man held up his hands in defense, "Because the throne is empty. Many more will try to come and claim the seat until, and even after the queen is officially crowned."

If Edric could breathe steam, he would certainly be close to that point right then and there. Madison being queen was important, yes. He wasn't doubting that. But someone literally tried to kill his woman.

Andreas calmly gripped his shoulder. "Easy, brother. I want to find out why as much as you do. But the old man has a point. We need to get that seat filled."

Edric settled his gaze on Andreas and his eyes widened and he backed away as well, also holding up his hands to ward off an attack.

He shook his head.

Two steps forward.

One step back.

CHAPTER THIRTY-ONE

SOPHIA

*S*ophia stood by, listening as the men bickered back and forth with the old man. Finally, she had enough.

"That's enough!" Her voice carried through the air.

All of the men, including the elder, settled their attentions on her.

"I should have a say in what happens next."

Edric opened his mouth to say something, but she snapped her hand up to stop him. He clamped his mouth shut.

"I adore that each of you are protective over me," she said, addressing her men, "but the elder is right. We set out to restore the heir to the throne. And seeing as how we are moments away from such a thing, I'm not stopping. Not even to solve the mystery of who wants me dead."

She looked toward Madison who stood by, watching the scene unfold. Her cousin nodded once. She took that as a sign to continue.

"Right now, the throne is empty. That essentially makes it up for grabs for anyone with the ambition to take it. The longer everyone stands around bickering only allows more of a chance for someone else to show up and create more problems."

She gave each of the men a pointed gaze, daring any of them to say otherwise. Satisfied that they were considering her words, she continued. "I have a feeling the attacks go much deeper than just an attempt at the throne. Someone in the mountain is after us, and we need to get Madison crowned so that the throne is secured. Then we can discuss the mountain assassins."

The men all nodded. She turned to the old man and said, "I'm Sophia Delmonte, Madison's cousin."

"I am Elder Pyre Velderdash. Very pleased to meet you, my lady." He bowed slightly at the waist.

Sophia felt awkward having someone not only call her lady, but bow to her when, most of the time, people would usually want to kill her first. But she was the cousin to the heir to Nighthelm's throne. She had better get used to it.

"What needs to be done?"

"Well…" his voice was aged, and his eyes were cloudy. "With Her Majesty's permission, I will take over the arrangements. In the following day, she is to be cleaned up, dress the part, and prepare for her new role as queen. Meanwhile, you will guard her and make sure no harm comes to her."

Sophia looked to Madison. "Well, Your Majesty, do we have your permission?"

She smiled. "Permission granted."

Sophia nodded and let out a deep breath as nervous energy pulsed through her. She had finally come to the point she had fought for. She will soon complete this stage of her destiny. She will finally restore the Nighthelm throne.

~

SOPHIA

*W*alking through the halls, Madison pointed out all their favorite hiding spots as children as they made their way toward the bedrooms. Sophia loved that she was learning more about her past, though it broke her heart that she couldn't remember on her own. Because her soul was purposefully broken. She tried to shake that feeling, though it always stayed just below the surface.

"Oh, so many fun memories," Madison said. "One day, we snuck into the kitchen and stole sweet cakes from the cook." She laughed. "He caught us, and chased us into the hallway, holding his spatula in the air. He was playing along, of course. But we hid right about..."

They took several steps as Madison held her finger out toward the wall to the left of the group. Sophia kept her eyes where the finger was pointing, wishing with everything in her that more than just familiarity would come to her.

"There!" Madison said.

It was an empty spot along the wall. Above it was a huge canvas with the image of the duchess painted on it. Sophia frowned. That painting would be the first to go.

"A small cabinet used to stand there. It was a family heirloom. We hid inside it, eating the sweets as the cook, who obviously had seen us, slowly walked by us saying, 'where'd those girls run off to?' We giggled and he would then say, 'just as well. The king would be very upset if the girls spoiled their dinner.' And he walked away."

Sophia laughed along with her cousin and her men.

"Can't imagine Sophia sneaking anything and laughing about it," Andreas said.

"How fun to learn of you as a little girl," Ezekiel said, earning a playful glare from Sophia.

Edric looked on, bemused. He seemed curious to know more, from the way he looked at Sophia. She couldn't blame him. She wanted to know more as well. She lived it. That much she knew deep inside her. But she couldn't pull the memory from her mind.

One of the housekeepers of the castle headed the group, leading them down the series of vast halls. She kept to herself as she ambled toward each individual room. She seemed rather solemn. Sophia stepped closer to her cousin. "That woman seems afraid. It would do your people good to talk to them. Address them as people and not powerless servants. They had been under duress for too long."

She nodded. "Excuse me."

The servant stopped and turned to face them, keeping her head down at all times. "Y-yes, Your Highness?"

Madison approached the woman and used the tips of her fingers to lift the woman's face up. "I'm not that dreadful woman. You don't have to cower any longer. You are able to make this your home, not your prison. Please, let me know what I can do to help with your comfort."

The woman made eye contact, tears brimming, making the browns of her irises glow like sunlight in the woods. "Thank you, Your Majesty! Thank you!"

"Tell us of your knowledge of the castle's set up. I'm curious to know what that woman had changed and what you would like to see restored."

She nodded. Sophia felt proud of her cousin. She

stood so tall. The way she interacted with her people showed she cared for them instead of seeing them as beneath her. The world needed more rulers like her.

Madison would make a great queen.

CHAPTER THIRTY-TWO

SOPHIA

*L*ater that night, in her new chambers, Sophia moved throughout the room fingering the expensive linens, running her fingers over the intricate designs on the wooden furniture, and taking in the elaborate space of the room that used to belong to part of her family.

And in essence, still did.

The sheer size of the room and the expensive furnishings were nearly overwhelming. She wondered if she would ever remember running through the halls as a young girl. It was different being in the castle without it attacking her. But it was also peaceful and freeing. She was relaxed for the first time in as long as she could remember.

She pondered how things had come full circle and

wondered if Madison could be as great a ruler as her uncle once was.

Of course, she would. She would be greater.

A knock on the door pulled her from her reverie. She answered with a soft, "Come in."

Edric stepped into the room, freshly bathed, bandaged, and wearing a clean uniform. He smiled as his eyes took in her form. After clearing his throat, he said, "I wanted to check in on you and make sure you were comfortable."

She nodded and softly smiled. "I am."

"Do you need anything?" he asked.

She shook her head and let her eyes roam over the vast, lavish room again. His feet shuffled and she set her attention on him as he went to leave.

"I may need one thing," she said, stopping him.

He faced her, eyebrows raised in arches on his forehead. "Anything."

"Stay with me," she said.

He lowered his head, obliging her. She met him halfway through the room and wrapped her arms around his waist, burying her face into his chest. His scent was intoxicating and eased the musings of her mind.

He pulled her closer into him, and she melted a little, wanting more of him.

She pulled him toward the bed as a gentle breeze blew in from the windows, making the curtains dance into the room. The bed that was far too big for just her seemed perfect for the two of them. He didn't need any coaxing, picking up on what she needed. And that was just to be comforted by him, being wrapped in his arms with his scent all around her.

She lay next to him, with her head on his chest. She listened to the beating of his heart and wrapped her fingers around the lace of his shirt. The fire in the nearby inglenook created soothing shadows and light and warmth.

She sighed as he placed a kiss on the top of her forehead.

Tomorrow, her cousin would be crowned queen. For now, she just wanted to relax and enjoy the peacefulness of not having to fight, feeling safe in the arms of her love.

CHAPTER THIRTY-THREE

SOPHIA

This was too much fussing for Sophia's taste. But her cousin, Madison, insisted on being pampered before the coronation. She cited something her mother always said, and Sophia couldn't recite it if her life depended on it.

Women—Sophia had lost count—danced through the room, performing random tasks while she relaxed in a steaming bath full of suds and flowery extracts. She loved the feel of the water against her aching muscles, and the soap stung a bit on her wounds, but she enjoyed the moment, nonetheless.

"Not bad, huh?" Madison asked from the bath next to hers.

Sophia shrugged. "This part isn't."

"Well, get used to it, Cousin. You are going to have this and so much more."

A weight formed in the pit of her stomach. Sophia didn't know if she was cut out for this to be a reoccurring thing. She had spent much of her life depending on herself, taking care of her own grooming, and wearing clothes that were meant for a warrior and not a lady.

"Let's just stick with today and call that good," she said.

"Why?" she asked, sitting forward in her bath and angling herself to face Sophia.

"It feels…" What word could she use to describe the feeling deep within her. The uncomfortable attention and pampering that most higher-class women took for granted but was never afforded to Sophia. She wasn't a lady. She wasn't raised with a silver spoon in her mouth, luxurious clothing, or even bubble baths. She was raised a fighter, an *anima contritum*. A thing that was never meant to exist, regardless if she was turned into one or not. She finally settled on a word. "Unusual."

"That's understandable," she said. "I feel that way too."

Sophia leveled her gaze on her cousin. "You do?"

She nodded. "Though I am used to being prepared for gatherings, despite a decade in a crystal coffin, I'm not used to addressing the kingdom. Honestly? I'm nervous. And a bit scared."

"Of being queen?" Sophia asked.

"Of letting my people down." Madison leaned back into the tub, holding up handfuls of bubbles and letting them drip from her hand. "There is so much to make up for. So much learning and catching up on events affecting my people. My father made it look so easy. I just hope that I am as good and as just as he was."

Sophia reached over the edge of her tub and grabbed her cousin's hand, pulling Madison's attention to her. With a smile she said, "You were born to lead these people. You are kind and strong. You have your father's blood within you. If not as great, you will be greater."

Madison beamed. "Thank you. For everything."

"It's what I do," Sophia said.

Then a woman poured fragrant water over her head, washed her hair, wrapped it in a thick cloth, and ordered her out of the bath. Sophia raised an eyebrow. This was too much pomp and circumstance. She wasn't used to it, and she felt uncomfortable with the trouble and lengths the number of women went through just to make sure she was dressed in luxury.

But she wouldn't give it up for the world.

SOPHIA

*T*he dress she wore didn't feel nearly as foreign as the one she had stolen from the duke she pretended was her uncle's house.

It was free flowing around the waist, hugged her hips just right, and supported her breasts comfortably. She could breathe freely as well. Her hair was pulled back and adorned with a silver diadem that held a small ruby dangling from the tip at the center of her forehead. Golden curls fell along her shoulders and dangled down her back.

She walked down the aisle of the chapel, the halls filled with people who once feared her, but now beamed with pride. They finally had their monarch on the throne once more. As the music of harps, violins, and flutes swelled, she held her chin high in defiance, doing her best to hide the broad smile that wanted to break free.

At the end of the aisle, Madison sat on a lavish throne, a temporary replacement to the one in the throne room as repairs were currently being done to restore it to its former glory. On her right was a smaller, backless seat. Next to it was Edric. To the left of her cousin stood Andreas and Ezekiel, each of them wore their most expensive dressings.

She climbed the few stairs of the dais and stood before her cousin who smiled. Regal in her red and gold dress.

Elder Velderdash nodded from the side as he grabbed the crown off a puffy pillow. He handed the crown to Sophia, and she once again faced Madison. As she placed the crown on her cousin's head, she couldn't hide the smile any longer.

She had done it.

She finally, officially, restored the heir.

But more than that, she truly had a family and home again.

She took her seat next to the queen as she addressed the people.

"People of Nighthelm, it is an honor to serve you as queen. And," she paused to look at Sophia, "my first act as queen is to officially pardon Sophia Delmonte, Edric Axton, Andreas Hilt, and Ezekiel Wickham of all charges and allegations brought against them."

As her cousin continued, Sophia slyly looked at her men. They beamed with pride in their own ways.

Madison finished her speech as the people began chanting her name.

Sophia Delmonte, the child of two nations, here to unite two worlds at war. She smiled at her cousin, faced the people and said, "Long live Queen Madison!"

The people repeated the chant. She bowed her head to her cousin and mouthed "thank you."

Madison bowed her head and looked at her people proudly.

Sophia had never been as happy as she was in this moment. She didn't want that feeling to end.

CHAPTER THIRTY-FOUR

SOPHIA

*S*ophia stood on her balcony overlooking the entire city below her. She watched as the lamps were being lit and wondered at the sight. She used to watch the lamp glow from the rooftops of the buildings or from within the shadows. Never once did she ever think she would stand on a balcony of the castle to experience the same thing.

From up here, it was like watching the birth of tiny fairies.

From just beyond the city, the red sun was setting along the horizon, spreading its final light over the world in shades of orange and yellow, fading into light blue that darkened into the navy of night above her.

A gentle breeze blew through her hair, bringing with it the crisp smell of drying leaves, warm fires, and the twang of evergreens along the mountain. She smiled to herself as she breathed in those scents.

This was what she had fought for. This moment. To have this peace. This accomplishment. She had fought long and hard for this moment. And she was doing all that she could to take it in.

The laughter of her men and casual chatter floated to her from within her room. She turned and found them heading toward the balcony where she stood. Edric carried a tray of fruits and cheeses. Ezekiel carried tall mugs, and Andreas held a carafe of wine.

When she met his gaze, he smiled and said, "We stole these from the kitchen. Sorry, there weren't any sweet cakes."

Edric added, "Or an angry cook to chase us down."

Sophia laughed and her men joined in.

While Andreas poured wine into the cups and passed them out, Sophia plucked a cube of cheese from the tray Edric placed on the wide edge of the balcony wall. She took a mug that was handed to her and waited until Ezekiel's was filled.

"A toast," she said, once everyone had their drinks.

"What are we toasting to now?" Andreas asked.

Ezekiel said, "To a destiny fulfilled, completed quests, lasting love, and a new peace."

"Wow, Zeke," Edric said. "How long did you rehearse that one?"

Sophia laughed. "I'll drink to that!"

Everyone clanked their mugs together and took a long pull of their wine.

Sophia faced the majestic Ripthorn Mountain. Her legacy. Her cousin was officially crowned the first Queen of Nighthelm from a family of a long line of kings. She had no doubt they would both leave their mark, each in their own way.

She relished in her victory, remembering her past, and seeing where she had come to. With her men, she restored the throne of Nighthelm. They deserved this moment of celebration and peace.

Sure, darkness waited for her within the depths of the mountain. Dark magic and shadows that won't be contained forever. If they could defeat the Nameless Master, they could face anything. She believed that more than ever. And the dangers in the mountain would prove a long fight, for certain.

But for now...

For the moment, at least, she can simply enjoy her victory.

"What comes next?" Ezekiel asked. "Do we stay here in the castle for a little while or head straight for the mountain to track those assassins?"

Sophia thought about that for a moment. "First, we will need a better way to keep you and Edric safe from magic poisoning. Then we head for the assassins."

"I would like to set up an elite force to guard the queen as well," Edric said.

"I like your thinking," Sophia said. "You can work on that. Zeke, you can research ways to recharge and reinforce the amulets the elder arbors gave you, and Andreas and I will help around the castle with repairs and wherever else we are needed."

Wind whipped through her hair blowing it into her face. Laughing with her men, she embraced each of them. She was grateful for them, for their power, and for the deep sense of wholeness she finally felt.

At long last, she was *healed*.

YOU'RE MISSING OUT...

Olivia Ash occasionally takes over the Wispvine Publishing social media channels on Facebook, Instagram, and Twitter.

Olivia also likes to hang out with Lila Jean in their Facebook group specifically for readers like you to come together and share their lives and interests, especially regarding the hot guys from their reverse harem novels. Please check it out and join in whenever you get the chance! Everyone in there is amazing, and you'll fit right in.

https://www.facebook.com/groups/LilaJeanOliviaAsh/

Sign up for email alerts of new releases AND exclusive access to bonus content, book recommendations, and more!

https://wispvine.com/newsletter/nighthelm-academy-email-signup/

Enjoying the series? Awesome! Help others discover The Nighthelm Guardian Series by leaving a review at Amazon.

http://mybook.to/Nighthelm1

ABOUT THE AUTHOR

OLIVIA ASH

Olivia Ash spends her time dreaming up the perfect men to challenge, love, and protect her strong heroines (who actually don't need protecting at all). Her stories are meant to take you on a journey into the world of the characters and make you want to stay there.

Reviews are the best way to show Olivia that you care about her stories and want other people discover them. If you enjoyed this novel, please consider leaving a review at Amazon. Every review helps the author and she appreciates the time you take to write them.